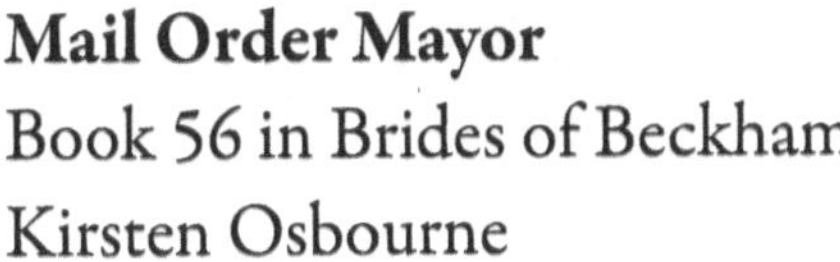

Mail Order Mayor

Book 56 in Brides of Beckham

Kirsten Osbourne

Chapter One

Rosabelle Winslow, known simply as Rosie, clasped her hands tightly in her lap, her sisters flanking her like steadfast sentinels. Elizabeth Tandy looked at the three sisters sitting side by side, Rosie with her blond hair, Izzy a brunette, and Ana the redhead. They were triplets, but though they did look like sisters, they weren't identical.

As a matchmaker, Elizabeth Tandy had spoken to them of traveling west and leaving town immediately, going to a town where three bachelors were looking for wives. She handed each sister a letter and waited as they read them.

As Rosie read her letter, she felt that it would better suit her sister Izzy, and Izzy had the same thought. They swapped their letters, and Rosie settled in to read the new letter in her hands, hoping this one would suit her better than the first.

June 1898

Dearest Madam,

As I pen this letter, I look out my window at the bustling streets of Hope Springs and the mountains that cradle our town. My name is Charles Jordan, and I have the honor of serving as the mayor of this vibrant town, a role that brings great responsibility. My two closest friends and I are all penning letters at the same time, hoping that we will all receive brides who are already friends.

Hope Springs is a place where individuals from all walks of life come together in pursuit of dreams.

In this role, I have dedicated myself to the welfare and prosperity of our community, guiding Hope Springs through the difficulties that mining towns often face. Yet, I find myself longing for a partner to share in the beauty and burdens of this life

I envision a woman of strength and grace, one who finds beauty in the rugged landscape of Colorado and the honest toil of its people. A lady whose heart beats in rhythm with the pioneering spirit of the West, and whose presence would bring light and warmth to the home we would build together. In her, I hope to find not just a wife but a true partner, someone to stand by my side as we forge a future filled with love, laughter, and the shared triumphs and trials that life inevitably presents.

My aspirations for our life together are humble yet filled with the promise of richness that comes not from the silver in the mines, but from the moments of connection and growth that we would nurture. From quiet evenings spent under the vast, starlit sky to lively gatherings with friends and neighbors, our life in Hope Springs would be one of deep community ties and the simple pleasures that make life truly meaningful.

If these words resonate with you, if you too dream of a life built on the foundations of love, partnership, and mutual respect, then I invite you to come to Hope Springs and marry me. Together, we could explore the vast tapestry of life in the West, hand in hand, heart to heart, building a legacy of love and leadership that will illuminate the pages of Hope Springs' history.

With an open heart and hopeful anticipation,

Charles Jordan

Mayor of Hope Springs

As Rosie read the letter again, more slowly this time, she realized that Charles's words spoke to her. She liked the idea of being his wife and helping him with his political aspirations.

"I think this is the man for me. I want to marry this Charles Jordan, mayor of Hope Springs, Colorado."

Laughter bubbled up between them, a shared acknowledgment of the absurdity and beauty of seeking love in such a manner. Yet as the laughter faded, a sense of purpose remained, as tangible as the letter now resting in Rosie's possession.

Within an hour, Rosie and her sisters were at the train station there in Beckham, Massachusetts, waiting for their train to board. Rosie couldn't stop looking around her, worried that their father would appear from behind every person, there to drag them back to the farm kicking and screaming if that's what it took.

She missed her mother with everything inside her, but she also knew her future was with her sisters and not the father who had so enjoyed taking his belt to each of his daughters, and even to his wife on occasion.

She shook her head and got the image of her father out of her mind. He was the past, and she was running toward her future. A future she and her sisters were determined to share out west. In Hope Springs.

After many days on the train, Rosie once again opened the letter and read it.

The words were penned in a strong, assertive hand seeming to leap from the page. Charles Jordan, the mayor of Hope Springs, wrote with an earnestness that captivated her, each sentence weaving the image of a man both grounded and seeking—a kindred spirit, perhaps.

She hoped she was what he was looking for because once she was in Hope Springs, she had nowhere else to go.

"Companionship and a shared journey," she murmured aloud. It was exactly what she wanted from Charles, the man she would soon marry. If they ever got to Hope Springs that was. She was tired of being on the train, and she wanted to reach her destination...with her sisters at her side.

A wistful smile graced Rosie's lips as she envisioned the mountains of Colorado, so different from the flat horizons she was used to. Hope Springs. The name alone promised something more than the stifling confines of her current world. Could she dare to dream of a place where her fiery independence would be cherished rather than chided?

Yet no sooner had the spark of adventure ignited than the looming shadow of doubt crept over her. To marry a man whose face she had never seen, whose touch was as foreign as the untamed West—was it bravery or foolishness? Rosie shook her head, trying to dislodge the trepidation that coiled like a snake around her heart.

"Love is a gamble at the best of times," she mused. This was not just a matter of the heart, but a negotiation of her very future.

"Change requires courage," Elizabeth had said, her assurance echoing in Rosie's mind. True enough, but it also demanded a certain recklessness—a willingness to step off the edge of the known world and hope for wings on the way down.

The silence of the room pressed against her, laden with expectation. Outside, the gentle hum of daily life in 1898 carried on, unaware of the crossroads at which one woman stood. Rosie took a deep breath, the scent of ink and anticipation mingling in her senses. A new life beckoned, a canvas blank and broad, hers for the taking—if only she dared reach for it.

"Elizabeth," Rosie began, her voice cutting through the thick silence of the parlor, "I will marry him." Her words were not just a whisper of consent but a declaration of intent. She lifted her chin, her gaze meeting Elizabeth's steady one, a silent pact forming between them in that look.

The matchmaker's lips curved upwards, a smile blooming like a desert flower after rain. "Bravery suits you," Elizabeth said.

"Thank you," Rosie managed, her hands now still, folded demurely atop her lap. "Your faith in me...it gives me strength."

"Strength is already there," Elizabeth returned. "All three of you have shown great strength in leaving your father's farm. Now you simply have to let it take you on the next step and see where it leads."

"Even all the way to Colorado?" Rosie said. It was a feeble attempt to lighten the load of her decision, yet Elizabeth chuckled—a low, knowing sound.

"Especially to Colorado," she affirmed. "Remember, love is the greatest adventure of them all."

"Then it's settled," Rosie said, her earlier trepidation transforming into a thrill that gave her energy. "We shall embark on this adventure, come what may."

"Come what may," Elizabeth said, pleased that the sisters were going to get away.

Only an hour passed before the sisters all took seats on the train that would take them to their new lives—and hopefully their new loves.

Rosie shook her head as she realized she was on the train and just remembered the time in Elizabeth's office. A smile tugged at the corners of Rosie's lips. With each thought of Hope Springs, the excitement kindled within her, warming her from the inside out. She envisioned herself stepping onto those dusty streets. There, she would no longer be a woman defined by her past but one who could forge her own destiny. Perhaps she'd tend a garden or stand by Charles's side as he navigated the tribulations of being mayor.

As the train chugged along, Rosie's anticipation grew with every passing mile. She sat by the window, watching the landscape change from the familiar sights of Massachusetts to the unknown.

Rosie's mind wandered to Charles, the mayor who had captured her curiosity from afar. She imagined their life together in the quaint town, picturing herself by his side as they faced the challenges and triumphs that lay ahead.

She could picture how it would be. Despite his initial aloofness, there would be a depth to his character that would come out the longer she was there. She wouldn't see him and know that he was the man she needed to complete her. No, it would be slower than that. More subtle. People who met and immediately fell in love were works of fiction, and she wanted a love that would last her entire life.

Lost in her thoughts, Rosie barely noticed when Izzy nudged her and pointed out the window. As she turned to look, a vast expanse of rugged mountains and sprawling valleys greeted her gaze. The breathtaking beauty of the untamed wilderness filled her with a sense of awe and wonder.

In that moment, Rosie knew that her life was about to change in ways she could never have imagined. The train slowed as it approached the station, and Rosie's heart fluttered with nervous excitement. Stepping onto the platform, she felt a rush of anticipation mingled with a touch of trepidation at the unknown future that awaited her in Hope Springs.

As the sisters gathered their belongings and followed the bustling crowd toward the town, Rosie couldn't shake off the feeling of being on the cusp of a new chapter in her life. The dusty streets of Hope Springs stretched before her, lined with quaint storefronts and bustling activity that spoke of a community united by both hardship and hope.

The three sisters stood together, waiting for the men who would soon be there to take them away from each other. First, Ana left with

Dr. Mercer, and though the man Ana was marrying looked very tired, she had a feeling they were a perfect match.

And then came Albert Thoreau with his perfectly tailored suit and his air of superiority. She worried a little bit for Izzy, but she knew her sister could take care of herself. They were all strong because they'd had to be. They'd taken many beatings for one another over the years. No more though. Their father was many states away with no idea where they were. It was better that way.

Left alone, Rosie stood watching the town for a few minutes before finding a bench and putting her things on it before sitting beside them. Rosie knew she could choose to be upset that Charles was late, but it was easier to imagine that he was doing important work for the town. Of course, the town would have to come first. He hadn't even met her yet.

She waited for almost an hour before she spotted him. Charles Jordan stood at the end of the platform, his gaze steady as he watched Rosie. There was a flicker of warmth in his eyes that surprised Rosie, a hint of vulnerability that mirrored her own emotions at that moment.

With each step closer to him, Rosie felt a surge of courage welling up inside her. The air crackled with anticipation as she finally stood face-to-face with Charles. His usual aloof demeanor seemed to soften in the golden glow of the setting sun, casting a warm light on his rugged features.

"Rosie," he began, his voice deep and resonant, "I'm glad you're finally here."

Rosie felt a rush of relief flood through her at his welcoming tone. She managed a small smile before replying, "I'm glad to be here, Charles. To start this new chapter together."

As they walked through the streets of Hope Springs, Rosie couldn't help but notice the subtle change in Charles's demeanor. The townspeople greeted them warmly, and Rosie felt a sense of belonging settle over her like a comforting blanket.

"We need to go to the church and get ourselves married first. I was told you were coming here with your sisters?" he asked, looking around to see if he spotted any other new women around.

"Dr. Mercer was waiting for Ana when the train pulled into the station. Izzy had to wait a few minutes for Mr. Thoreau, but they've been gone a long while as well. It was nice having time to just sit and watch the town and get used to its rhythms," Rosie said softly.

Charles frowned and pulled out his pocket watch. "I had no idea it was so late. I had thirty minutes before your train pulled in, and then I decided to read one last document before signing it and come here to the station. I lost track of time, and I'm sorry for that, Rosabelle."

Rosie smiled. "Everyone calls me Rosie. My sisters and I were born Anabelle, Isabelle, and Rosabelle, but all our names were shortened quickly."

"I'll keep that in mind. Rosie."

"Do you have a nickname?" she asked as they approached the church.

Charles shook his head. "No, I've always been known as Charles."

They stepped into the church, and the pastor was at the front eating something with a young woman, and a baby who was sleeping on the floor.

As soon as they spotted the pastor, Charles called out to him. "I'm so sorry! I was late to the train station to pick up Rosabelle—Rosie."

The pastor put down the plate of food beside the woman who must be his wife. "Promptness doesn't seem to be in your vocabulary, Mr. Mayor."

Charles sighed. "Not for lack of trying!"

Rosie smiled. "Perhaps I can help keep you on schedule. I wouldn't mind," she said sweetly.

"I believe I can manage that on my own," Charles said, sounding slightly annoyed.

"All right then," Rosie said, unsure what she'd done to upset him, but she was sure she was just reading him wrong. She needed to stop trying to figure out what he was thinking.

The pastor rose and they had a five-minute wedding. It was enough time to speak their vows, and that was all they really needed. When the pastor invited Charles to kiss her, her new husband brushed his lips against her cheek instead of kissing her lips. But that was all right with Rosie. She was going to fall in love with him slowly, so she needed time before they kissed.

Everything was happening according to plan. She couldn't be happier.

Chapter Two

Charles offered Rosie his arm as they began the trek to his homestead. The path wound through groves of trees. Rosie's wide eyes roamed over the landscape, drinking in the sight of distant mountains. She marveled at the wildflowers that seemed to welcome her to this new life.

"Beautiful, isn't it?" Charles asked, his voice betraying a hint of pride.

"Oh, yes," Rosie replied. "I hope I never look around me and take the scenery for granted."

Charles chuckled, a sound that seemed out of place. "If it ever seems like you are, I'll find a stick and poke you with it."

Rosie couldn't help but giggle. It sounded like something her mother would have said, and as much as she missed her mother, it felt good to be reminded. So good.

As they crested the final rise, the homestead came into view. It was a sturdy structure that looked as if it could survive harsh winters and blistering summers. But as they approached, Rosie saw that the house had been neglected. Dust stained the windows, and cobwebs clung to the eaves like tattered lace.

"Here we are," Charles said, gesturing toward the house with a sweep of his hand.

Rosie stepped inside and was greeted by a kitchen that seemed to have been abandoned mid-meal and left to the mercy of time. A fine layer of dust coated every surface, and pots and pans lay scattered, bearing the crusty remnants of meals long past. The entire kitchen smelled sour.

"Seems I've got my work cut out for me," Rosie said, rolling up her sleeves. She was thrilled to know she was needed. "Can't start supper with the kitchen in this state."

"Apologies," Charles murmured. "It's been some time since anyone took care of the place."

"Then it's high time someone did," Rosie replied with a smile.

She filled a bucket with water drawn from the pump outside. She was no stranger to housework, and though she'd rather bake any day, she was happy to have a purpose here. As she scrubbed at the grime, the soapy water turned murky with neglect. The task was arduous, but Rosie found satisfaction in the way the room slowly transformed under her care. Here, at least, she could make a difference.

"Looks like you've done this before," Charles observed from the doorway.

"Many times," Rosie said, dipping a rag into the bucket. "Though I confess, I never imagined doing so in my own home."

"Your home," Charles repeated softly. "It's growing late, and I'm getting hungry."

Rosie knew Ana would have told him that supper would have long since been over if the kitchen had been clean, but she wasn't her sister. "I'll get it as soon as the kitchen is clean enough to cook in. Is there a restaurant in town you could go to, and I'll just make myself something when I'm done?"

Charles sighed. "You're here so I don't have to eat at the diner so much."

Rosie sat back on her heels. "The way I see it, you have two choices. You can wait until I'm finished and can cook for you, or you can go to the restaurant."

"I'll wait."

With each swipe of her cloth, Rosie uncovered more of the kitchen's potential, imagining the meals she'd prepare and the warmth she'd infuse into this space. She so loved it when the house smelled like something had just been baked.

"Better?" she asked, standing back to survey her handiwork.

"Much," Charles agreed.

"Supper won't be grand tonight," Rosie warned, her cheeks flushed with exertion. "But it'll be made with care."

"That's all I can ask for," said Charles, his gaze lingering on her longer than necessary before retreating back to the safety of distance. He'd married a very beautiful woman...again. Why hadn't he specified an ugly woman in his letter?

Rosie cracked the last egg into the sizzling skillet, the rich aroma of frying bacon mingling with the smell of cleanser still lingering in the air. She had found the larder nearly barren, save for these few staples. Staring at the cast-iron pan, she wished for bread to sop up the yolks, but there was none to be had.

"Supper's almost ready," she called over her shoulder, feeling a curious blend of domesticity and independence.

Charles sat at the head of the rough-hewn table, his chair creaking as he leaned back, watching her with an intensity that made her hands fumble with the spatula. "It smells good," he said, his deep voice carrying a note of genuine appreciation that warmed Rosie more than the heat from the stove.

"Thank you," she replied, her cheeks tinged with a rosy glow. She plated the food with care, setting down the heavy dishes with a clatter that seemed too loud in the quiet space between them.

As they began to eat, Charles cleared his throat, a sure sign he was about to impart something of importance. "I reckon I should tell you more about what keeps me busy," he started, piercing a piece of bacon with his fork. "I got a large herd of cattle, which means most of my time is spent out on the range."

Rosie nodded, silently urging him to continue as she took a careful bite of her egg.

"And besides that," he continued with a smile, "I have the town business to attend to." It was only the second time she'd seen him smile, and it made Rosie's heart flutter. "That's why I have five ranch hands to help out. You needn't worry about them. They tend to their own meals."

"That's a relief," Rosie said. Her mind raced with visions of town functions and political gatherings.

As they ate, Rosie found herself studying the lines of his face, the stern set of his jaw that softened when he spoke of his work, the subtle furrow of concentration between his brows. He was a man of many layers, she decided.

"Busy as I am," Charles said, breaking into her thoughts, "it's crucial to have someone looking after the homestead. Someone who understands the value of hard work and...companionship."

"Companionship," Rosie repeated, letting the word roll off her tongue as she contemplated its implications. She would stand by this man and share in his public life.

As Rosie was doing dishes, Charles walked into the kitchen to speak with her. "Rosie," Charles began. She turned, drying her hands on the apron tied around her waist, and found him leaning against the doorframe, his expression unreadable.

"Yes, Mr. Jordan?" she responded, noting how the shadows played across his rugged features.

"Please, call me Charles," he corrected gently, then cleared his throat. "I think it's time we lay our cards on the table."

"Of course, Charles." Rosie's heart picked up its pace, not from exertion but from the intensity gathering in his steel-blue eyes.

"I sent for you with a clear purpose in mind," he continued, his words deliberate. "I'm not looking for roses and romance, Rosie. I need someone to stand beside me at town functions, to keep my house, cook meals...someone who understands the value of partnership without the entanglement of love."

"Entanglement," she asked, wondering who had hurt him so much.

"Indeed." He paused, his gaze drifting toward the wall where a portrait hung—a woman with kind eyes and a soft smile. "My late wife, Margaret. She passed on a few years ago. It left a void, one that can't be filled nor should anyone try. What I am offering is a practical arrangement, nothing more."

Rosie felt a pang in her chest, a twinge of empathy for the man before her. She saw the subtle tremble in his hand as it brushed the back of the chair, a sign of vulnerability he quickly masked.

"Charles," she said, her voice steady, "I believe you loved your wife deeply. To live without her..." She trailed off.

"More than I can bear," he admitted in a whisper so faint, it was almost carried away by the wind that whistled through the cracks of the old homestead.

Rosie nodded, feeling an unexpected kinship with this stoic man. She respected his honesty, the raw edge of his sorrow that he worked so diligently to keep sheathed. They were both seeking something in this arrangement.

"Understood, Charles. You have my word—I'm here to help, not to replace."

A ghost of a smile touched his lips, a fleeting moment of gratitude that softened the hard lines of his face. "Thank you, Rosie. That means more to me than you might realize."

And Rosie was content. She would be married to a man who would be her lifelong companion, and she would do everything she could to make him happy. There was no need for love, though she was certain it would come. With time.

Rosie followed Charles, an oil lamp clasped in his hand lighting their way. They arrived at a door, slightly ajar, its paint chipped and bearing evidence of many years of use. He pushed it open with a gentle nudge of his elbow and stepped aside, allowing her to enter first.

"Your room," he said simply, gesturing into the modest space.

"Thank you, Charles," Rosie replied, crossing the threshold to survey her new sanctuary. A brass bedstead stood against one wall with its covers rumpled. A sense of purpose surged within her as she imagined transforming this neglected chamber into a haven of comfort. The only thing missing was her sisters.

Charles lingered awkwardly in the doorway, the lines of his face etched with the day's fatigue. "I'll leave you to settle in. Goodnight, Rosie."

"Goodnight." Her voice was soft but carried the steel of her resolve. She did not mind the separation of their rooms. One day they would be together, she was certain, but for now, she understood Charles still loved his first wife.

As his footsteps retreated down the hall, Rosie closed the door and exhaled, her breath mingling with the stale air of the room. With determined strides, she moved to the bed, stripping away the dusty linens with brisk efficiency. Underneath, the mattress bore the imprint of time but promised rest for weary bones.

Once satisfied with the bedroom's improved state, Rosie ventured into Charles's room. The sight of his dwelling tugged at her heartstrings—a stark realm devoid of feminine touch. She worked silently, methodically, her hands smoothing out creases on his bedspread, erasing remnants of solitude that clung stubbornly to the fabric.

Fluffing a pillow, a chuckle escaped her lips, acknowledging the absurdity of her situation—here she was, Rosabelle Winslow Jordan, a mail-order bride playing housemaid in a stranger's home. Yet the act of cleaning, of bringing order to chaos, filled her with a sense of accomplishment, of belonging.

Rosie tiptoed through the shadowed parlor, her heart thumping gently with the newness of the house at night. The soft glow of moonlight filtered through the window, casting a silver hue over the furniture that Charles had likely chosen with his late wife.

"Charles?" Her voice was a whisper, half-hoping he'd already surrendered to slumber. There was no answer, only the silent affirmation that the man had retreated to the solitude of his own room. She was surprised they hadn't passed one another in the hall. Perhaps he'd just gone to the outhouse? A curious blend of relief and disappointment fluttered in her chest. She had wanted to bid him goodnight.

With Charles's absence noted, Rosie's attention turned to the business of getting clean. The kitchen, with its rough-hewn counters and the lingering scents of their simple supper, offered sanctuary. She spied the bathtub tucked away under the workbench—a humble basin, hardly fit for luxury, but promising the comfort of warmth against her skin.

Water sloshed as she poured bucket after bucket, steam rising and mingling with the cool air of the kitchen. She undressed with an efficiency born of necessity, leaving her garments folded neatly on the chair beside the stove. Slipping into the hot embrace of the bath, Rosie closed her eyes and exhaled, the heat seeping into her weary bones.

It was during this moment of blissful solitude that the door creaked open. Charles stood there, framed by the doorway, his features sharpening as his eyes adjusted to the dim light. His breath caught at the sight before him—Rosie, with her fair skin, hair piled atop her head in a loose knot.

"Rosabelle," he began, the name tumbling out in a hushed reverence he hadn't intended.

"Charles!" Rosie's eyes snapped open, her hands instinctively reaching for the water's surface to preserve her modesty. "I—I thought you were asleep."

"Apologies, I—" He stumbled back, color rising to his cheeks. The image of her, so serene, so unexpectedly enchanting, seared itself into his mind. It wasn't what he had envisioned when he requested a bride.

Yet here she was, defying his plans with her unadorned beauty, stirring something within him that felt perilously close to longing.

"Goodnight, Rosie." His words were clipped, a feeble attempt to regain composure as he retreated hastily to his room, the door closing with a soft click behind him.

The silence settled once more, leaving Rosie blinking against the stark contrast of the warm water and the sudden chill of isolation. She let out a shaky laugh, finding humor in the absurdity of it all—their mutual surprise, the unspoken tension, the dance of propriety they both seemed eager to maintain.

"Goodnight, Charles," she whispered to the empty space, a smile playing on her lips. With a gentle sigh, Rosie submerged herself once more, allowing the water to wash away the embarrassment.

Under the heavy quilt, Charles shifted restlessly, his body tense as he tried to find a comfortable position. The mattress creaked under his weight. Each time he closed his eyes, the vision of Rosie bathed in the warm glow of the kitchen lantern flashed across his mind.

"Damnation," he muttered under his breath, turning onto his side with a huff. He was supposed to have married a plain woman, one who wouldn't stir these relentless yearnings. He had chosen practicality over passion, responsibility over romance. Yet, here she was, Rosie, inadvertently unraveling all his well-laid plans with her quiet grace.

He wanted to touch her, to know the warmth of her skin beneath his fingertips, but such thoughts were treachery against his late wife's memory. He clenched his jaw, frustration mounting. Why couldn't Rosie have been plain? It would have made everything simpler, and easier to bear.

But she wasn't, and as the night dragged on, Charles found no reprieve from his desires. But if he only knew one thing about life, he knew that he couldn't allow another woman to know he desired her. He wouldn't go through that again.

"Confound it all," he whispered into the darkness.

Chapter Three

osie's eyes fluttered open. Her body protested the early rise but she pushed the quilt aside with a sense of purpose that was new and invigorating. She slipped into her worn boots and tiptoed through the still house, careful not to wake Charles, who was likely exhausted.

The chill Colorado air nipped at Rosie's cheeks as she stepped outside, sending a cascade of goosebumps down her arms. It was still dark outside, but Rosie was determined to be the best wife she could be, and there was so much to be done.

Rosie made her way toward the henhouse, her steps light on the dew-kissed grass. She'd always taken comfort in these simple tasks, the kind that connected her to the earth. She'd loved planting, weeding, and harvesting the kitchen garden her mother had kept back home.

She knew she should probably be sadder than she was about her mother's death, but she chose to remember every minute with her mother with a smile. Every little thing that reminded Rosie of Mother caused happy feelings, not sad.

She and her sisters would have left home much earlier than they did if their mother hadn't been there for them. They'd stayed for her. Rosie couldn't count the times she or one of her sisters had gotten between their father's fist or belt and their mother. Keeping her safe had become one of the most important things she could do.

She unlatched the door and peered inside, where a few hens clucked on their perches. Rosie coaxed them aside to gently gather the eggs they'd left nestled in the straw. Her fingers were deft and used to farm work. A ranch wouldn't be a great deal different.

With her apron cradling the eggs, Rosie returned to the kitchen. She set a cast-iron skillet on the stove, the bacon sizzling as it hit the hot surface. There was no meat greater than bacon in her mind, and she hadn't had it nearly enough. Next, she whisked the eggs, pouring them into the pan where they began to dance and bubble into a fluffy scramble.

As the eggs cooked, Rosie found herself humming a tune her mother used to sing, the melody intertwining with the sounds of breakfast.

Rosie plated the food and poured two cups of coffee, setting the table with care. Maybe, just maybe, this simple breakfast would be the beginning of something new. Perhaps it would be the first step toward a true partnership.

Rosie allowed herself a small smile. For now, she had eggs to serve, and a day full of possibilities ahead. Maybe Charles wouldn't fall in love with her in the next week, but she had no doubt he would within the next decade. She wasn't a child. She could wait.

Rosie noticed it immediately—the way Charles's gaze looked away from hers. He busied himself with the cuff of his shirt, adjusting and readjusting a button that was already perfectly in place. The air between them was thick with the unsaid, filled with the echoes of last night's accidental encounter in the kitchen when she had been in the bath.

"Good morning, Charles," she said, her voice a soft melody meant to smooth over the wrinkled fabric of his embarrassment.

"Rosie," he replied, his tone clipped, but not unkind. His eyes finally met hers, a brief flicker before darting away to focus on something, anything else. "You're...up early."

"Couldn't sleep," Rosie said with a shrug that felt heavier than she intended. "I wanted to get breakfast done early. I should be able to get a lot of cleaning done today."

"We have church this morning," he told her, looking surprised she hadn't mentioned it already.

"Oh, will we attend church?" she asked.

"Yes, of course. Why wouldn't we? Didn't you go to church when you were in Massachusetts?"

"Mother took us when we were small, but then Father forbade us to go anywhere when we were five. So we never went to church again. Mother read to us from the Bible, and we're all Christians, but we just never had the opportunity to go to church."

"That's sad," he said, frowning. The more he learned about her childhood, the more he disliked her father.

She shrugged. "I had my two best friends sharing a room with me. While Father worked, Mother taught us to read, write, and do arithmetic. My childhood was a good one." *When my father wasn't beating my mother or one of my sisters.* She hadn't minded as much when he hit her, but she'd hated it when someone she loved was the one being abused.

"All right," he said. He wasn't going to argue with her about how her childhood had been, but it sounded miserable to him.

She took her seat across from him and offered him the bowl of pepper. "I don't think I put enough on the eggs, but I wasn't sure how much you like."

"Thank you," he murmured. Taking the bowl and spoon from her hand, he added a liberal amount of pepper, aware that she was watching him closely.

Finally, Charles cleared his throat, a determined set to his jaw as he finally looked up at her.

"Make sure you wear something pretty for church."

Rosie frowned. "I can only wear the dresses I have. If you want pretty, it's time for me to make something new."

She and her sisters would be the three worst-dressed women there. She had no doubt. But it didn't matter. She would see her sisters!

"You'll need to make something new then." Charles shook his head. "We should leave soon. Wouldn't want to be late."

Rosie rose from her seat with a sense of purpose. They were to be seen together, the mayor and his new bride, playing their parts for the town. She hoped that under the watchful eyes of their neighbors, they could find a moment of genuine connection.

Rosie's heart fluttered as the wooden doors of the church swung open, ushering in a shaft of sunlight that seemed to pierce through the weight of her uncertainties. The pews were a sea of Sunday bests and hopeful faces, but among them, there was only one she sought.

"Charles," she said, clutching his arm, "I do believe I see my sister."

Before he could offer any word of caution or concern, Rosie had already hurried away. When her eyes finally found Izzy, they sparkled with joy.

"Izzy!" Rosie embraced her sister. "I've been so eager to see you."

"And how is married life treating you?"

"Oh, Charles is a dear," Rosie confided. "He's sweet and ever so kind." Though she wished for more, she didn't want her sisters to know. Not yet, anyway.

"Is he now?" Izzy raised an eyebrow.

"Truly, he is," Rosie insisted, though the words carried the weight of incompleteness—a story untold, a book with pages still unturned.

The murmur of the gathering crowd hushed as another figure approached, and Rosie's eyes lit up anew. Ana joined them, hugging them each in turn.

"Ana!" Rosie's exclamation was a soft gasp of delight. "It feels like years since we've all been together."

"It's been less than twenty-four hours," Izzy said, shaking her head.

"It *did* feel longer," Ana said. "But here we are, under God's grace and each other's gaze."

"Isn't it wonderful?" Rosie beamed, her hands clasping those of her sisters. "Just like old times, only...different."

"Better," Izzy chimed in, "because now we're three strong women, each with a husband of our own."

"Yes," Ana agreed. "And we'll figure out how to be good wives. We have no choice."

As the bell called them to worship, the sisters stood shoulder to shoulder. Each of them hurried to find her husband and join him for service.

Rosie glanced sideways at Charles, standing stoically at the end of the row. Perhaps this public display of unity could ignite a private connection yet. For now, she picked up a hymnal and did her best to sing along.

After the service concluded, Rosie was thrilled to join her sisters again.

"Shall we dine together?" Dr. William Mercer proposed, his gaze sweeping over the group.

"An excellent idea," Albert Thoreau agreed.

As they walked, Rosie watched Albert, thinking there was something not quite right for Izzy about him, but she couldn't put her finger on what it was. Her sister looked happy enough, but there was sadness in her eyes.

Charles, standing a trifle apart, gave a small nod before his gaze met Rosie's. She smiled at him, taking his arm with her hand. He wanted a wife in public, and he was going to get one.

The three couples settled at a robust wooden table near the window of the diner. Laughter punctuated the meal as stories were swapped, and Charles's occasional smiles, though fleeting, did not go unnoticed by Rosie.

As plates were cleared and cups of coffee served, the conversation turned to plans for the following day. Izzy, her eyes sparkling with mischief, leaned forward.

"Tomorrow, let's meet at the general store after lunch," she suggested. "I've been dying to make a new dress, and I can't imagine doing it without you two."

"Indeed," Ana said, her practicality always at the helm. "It's high time we add some fresh stitches to our wardrobes. What do you say, Rosie?"

"Nothing would please me more," Rosie replied, the prospect of shared sisterly endeavors warming her like the afternoon sun.

"Let's each pick a different color," Izzy chirped, already lost in visions of vibrant fabrics.

"Of the same pattern," Ana added, ever the organizer.

"Perfect," Rosie sighed contentedly.

William chuckled softly. "I suspect the general store won't know what hit it when the Winslow sisters descend."

"Nor will Charles, once he sees the bill," Albert jested, earning a playful glare from his friend.

"Whatever my wife desires," Charles stated, a touch of warmth seeping into his voice as his glance slid briefly to Rosie.

"Then it's settled," Izzy declared, her smile as wide as the prairie sky. "Tomorrow, we create!"

With cups emptied and farewells exchanged, the party dispersed, each couple stepping out into their separate lives. Yet, for Rosie, the promise of tomorrow was a thread pulling her heart toward a future rich with possibilities.

LATER, HOME WITH CHARLES, Rosie thought about what cleaning project she should tackle first.

"Rosie," Charles said suddenly, "there is something I should show you." His tone held a note of formality that piqued her curiosity. With a courteous hand at her elbow, he led her toward the house and then veered off toward the cellar door.

"Most folks keep their ice boxes in the kitchen or pantry," he explained as he opened the door, revealing the wooden steps descending into cooler shadows. "But Margaret—my wife—she believed it would be better down here, where the air stays cold."

"Practical," Rosie murmured, trailing behind him, her boots echoing softly on the stairs. The cellar held rows of preserved goods and neatly stacked firewood, but what caught her eye was the large ice box sitting against the far wall.

"Quite," Charles agreed with a nod. "She was always full of such notions."

As he opened the box to reveal its chilly contents, Rosie leaned forward, her breath forming a faint mist. There, nestled among the blocks of ice, lay an assortment of meats, vegetables, and dairy products. Her hands reached for a cut of beef, envisioning the rich aroma of stew bubbling over the fire.

"Supper," she announced.

"All right," he replied, his words clipped.

With arms laden with provisions, Rosie climbed back up to the warmth of the kitchen. As she set about preparing the meal, she couldn't help but wonder at the oddities of marriage.

Soon, the stew simmered, fragrant and hearty. Rosie watched Charles from the corner of her eye as he pretended not to notice the way she moved around the kitchen that had been his first wife's, now hers by both right and necessity, transforming raw ingredients into a meal that spoke of home.

ROSIE WAS ALREADY AWAKE before there were any signs of morning the following day. She dressed quickly, tying her apron tight around her waist, a determined glint in her eye. Today, she would spend the afternoon with her sisters, a reunion of hearts and laughter. But first, there were chores to be done, a testament to the endless rhythm of domestic life.

She gathered the laundry. With practiced ease, she plunged each item of clothing into the wash basin, scrubbing and rinsing until her fingers pruned. One by one, she pinned the garments to the line.

In the kitchen, she started breakfast. The coffee pot gurgled happily, sending forth tendrils of steam that fogged the windowpanes.

"Good morning," Charles greeted, his voice groggy with sleep. He eyed the spread with appreciation, though his gaze lingered only briefly on Rosie before skittering away.

"Morning," she replied, her tone chipper despite the early hour.

"I'll be with my sisters this afternoon. Perhaps we can invite them as well as their husbands for supper soon?" Rosie asked, pouring the coffee with a steady hand.

Charles paused, his fork midway to his mouth. "I have...duties," he said.

"Of course," she nodded. She was happy her sisters had married friends of his because he would be much more likely to be willing to have them around.

She gathered the soiled bedding from Charles's room. She was methodical as she plunged the fabrics into the soapy water, her arms working with the kind of fervor found only in those who understand the value of hard-earned cleanliness.

Rosie tackled the pantry while the clothes on the line dried. She scrubbed at the floorboards until they shone, and the walls—once dulled by layers of dust—now gleamed.

"Rosie Jordan does not shy away from elbow grease," she muttered to herself, a wry smile playing on her lips.

Later that afternoon, Rosie met her sisters at the general store. Her heart swelled at the sight of them. Never in her life had she spent more than a few hours without the company of either sister, and life felt so different without them. No one who wasn't a multiple could ever understand the bond between her and her sisters.

"Rosie!" Izzy called out.

Minutes later, they were all in the store, looking at the bolts of fabric the store had to offer.

"Look at these patterns," Ana said.

Yet it was the simple calico print that caught their collective gaze—a delicate floral motif that seemed to whisper of springtime promises and sisterly bonds.

"Let's all make a dress out of this one," Rosie proposed, tracing the outline of a petal with her fingertip. "Each in a different color."

"We won't be identical like Mother always preferred, but people will know we're a unit," Izzy said as she selected cream colored fabric with the pretty ivy for her dress.

"Reminds me of when we were little, twirling around the parlor in matching frocks," Ana said, reaching for a green bolt.

And so it was decided. Rosie picked out a warm shade of rose, her namesake color. It was more than mere fabric; it was a tapestry of kinship, of shared laughter and whispered secrets beneath the quilt of stars that blanketed their childhood nights.

As they made their purchases, Rosie couldn't help but feel a tug at her heartstrings—a pull toward the past mingled with the thrill of forging new memories.

"When we're done," Rosie declared, "we'll be as sisters reborn, each a reflection of the other, yet uniquely ourselves."

THE AROMA OF BAKING sugar and butter wafted through the air as Rosie, Izzy, and Ana bustled around the kitchen in a symphony of sisterly cooperation. Ana's house was filled with activity. The oven, stoked to a steady heat, stood ready to transform their efforts into golden morsels of sweetness.

After they'd finished their tea and cookies, they all sat down to work on their dresses.

"Rose suits you," Ana said, glancing at her sister with approval.

"New beginnings," Rosie mused, her heart fluttering at the thought. She had come here as Charles's bride, but she still felt like a little girl.

As their scissors snipped and their needles danced, the patterns began to take shape. They chatted about everything and nothing, the hum of their voices a comforting blanket that wrapped around them. They spoke of the townsfolk, of the miners, and Elizabeth Tandy, whose matchmaking skills had set them on this path.

"I never imagined myself a lazy wife with a rich husband," Izzy said, her needle pausing mid-stitch.

"Nor I as a mayor's," Rosie replied, her gaze meeting Ana's. "But here we are, defying expectations."

"Speaking of expectations," Ana quipped, "let's make sure these dresses fit well enough to impress our respective gentlemen." She winked, and Rosie couldn't help but chuckle.

"Ah yes, because heaven forbid, we don't uphold societal expectations in our attire," Rosie said, rolling her eyes playfully.

"William will be pleased with whatever I wear. He's such a kind man," Ana said.

Izzy looked uncomfortable but said nothing.

Chapter Four

Rosie walked beside Charles. "Look there," she pointed toward a hawk soaring above them, its cry piercing the silence. "Freedom must feel like that, don't you think?" She'd had her first taste of freedom the night she and her sisters had left the farm where they grew up.

Charles followed her gaze, a smile tugging at the corners of his mouth. "Perhaps. But even the hawk must return to the nest."

"Then I hope he has someone warm waiting for him," Rosie said, a playful lilt in her voice. When Charles allowed himself to relax, which didn't happen often, Rosie found him downright charming and fun to be around.

As the trail took a lazy turn, they stumbled upon an unexpected treasure: a hidden meadow bursting with wildflowers, a riot of colors set against the green canvas of Hope Springs. Rosie's breath caught in her throat at the sight, her heart suddenly racing in her chest.

"Would you look at that," Charles murmured.

"Like something out of a fairy tale," Rosie whispered back, stepping into the clearing, her hands itching to touch the blooms.

Together, they knelt among the flowers, fingers grazing as they plucked stems and wove them into a bouquet. Rosie's pulse quickened each time their skin touched, a jolt of electricity that seemed to charge the air around them. She watched as Charles selected a beautiful rose-hued bloom, his hand steady despite the way his eyes darted up to meet hers with an intensity that left her breathless.

"Here," he said, his voice low, "this one should be the centerpiece."

"Because it's the brightest?" Rosie teased, taking the flower from him, careful not to let her fingers linger over his.

"Because it stands out, just like you," Charles replied, the honesty in his voice wrapping around her like a warm embrace.

Amid the wildflower meadow, Rosie realized that Hope Springs had more magic to offer than just picturesque views. It was here, in the simple act of creating together, that Rosie saw glimpses of the man Charles hid behind his mayoral façade—a man capable of passion and humor.

"Thank you, Charles," Rosie said softly, holding the burgeoning bouquet to her chest. "For this."

"Thank you, Rosie," Charles said, his gaze unwavering, "for making everything seem new."

Their shared smiles were like secrets whispered between kindred spirits, promises of deeper connections yet to be explored in the quaint town of Hope Springs, where love began to blossom among the wildflowers.

DAYS LATER, ROSIE PREPARED for their evening. She arranged the table in the backyard, her hands working diligently to create an ambiance filled with romance and starlight.

"Rosie?" Charles's voice carried a note of surprise. He had expected a simple supper, not an alfresco dining experience under the celestial tapestry of the night sky.

"Surprise," she said, her eyes shining with mischief and delight. "I thought we'd enjoy the stars tonight." Even though she knew he wasn't quite ready to forget about Margaret, she did her best to put them into situations where they were more likely to fall for each other.

They sat, knees almost touching, plates generously filled. Laughter mingled with the clinking of cutlery, each joke, each shared memory bringing them closer. Charles regaled her with tales of Hope Springs' eccentricities, while Rosie's wit sparked laughter that rang clear as the crisp Colorado air.

"Your laugh," Charles said, pausing, a smile tugging at his lips, "it's quite infectious."

"Only because your stories are so amusing, Mr. Mayor," Rosie teased back, her eyes sparkling with humor.

The meal concluded, and they lingered over dessert, neither ready to end their evening. Rosie's heart fluttered like the wings of a hummingbird as she noticed the way Charles's gaze lingered on her lips.

"Rosie," he began, his voice a low murmur that seemed to resonate with the thrum of the night, "I—"

"Shh," she interrupted, placing a finger gently upon his lips, her own heart daring to hope. "Let's just sit here, under the stars."

Rosie leaned her head against Charles's shoulder, and for the first time, the distance between them felt like nothing at all.

CHARLES LED ROSIE THROUGH the bustling Hope Springs town fair, his hand firm on her elbow, a rare touch that sent a pleasant shiver up her spine. The vibrant colors of the stalls, the jovial calls of the vendors, and the laughter of children darting between the legs of adults lent an air of joy that was impossible to resist.

"Rosie," Charles said suddenly, halting before a ring toss booth, "I bet I can land more rings than you."

His eyes gleamed with a playful challenge, one she hadn't seen before. It was as if the spirit of the fair had infused him with a light-hearted boldness that surprised and delighted her.

"Is that so, Mr. Mayor?" Rosie teased, accepting the gauntlet thrown at her feet. "Prepare to be humbled."

They squared off, their competitive streaks igniting as each took turns tossing rings, the clang of metal on wood punctuating their attempts. Rosie's accuracy earned her a small cheer from onlookers, but it was Charles who triumphed, a boyish grin spreading across his face as he claimed a stuffed bear prize.

"Victory is sweet," he crowed, presenting it to her with an exaggerated flourish.

"Only because you're not used to it," Rosie quipped back, unable to suppress her own smile. She accepted the bear, tucking it under her arm like a badge of honor.

Their laughter subsided as they strolled away from the games toward the quieter edge of the fair. Here, away from the cacophony, Rosie saw a different side of Charles emerge—a softer, thoughtful expression.

"Did you ever dream of something different, Charles?" Rosie ventured, her voice low. "Before becoming mayor, I mean."

He stopped, facing her, his gaze holding a depth she'd seldom glimpsed. "When I was a boy, I dreamed of being a rancher," he confessed, "and being the first rancher to raise buffalo." His chuckle was self-deprecating. "Foolish dreams of a young mind."

"Those dreams sound wonderful, not foolish," Rosie encouraged, touched by his candor. "How did a man who dreamed of being a buffalo rancher become a mayor anyway?"

He took a deep breath. "John Thompson wanted to be mayor. He's not a good man, Rosie, and when William, Albert, and I talked of him running unopposed, they decided I was the best man for the job. John, Albert, and I all made our fortunes in the silver mines. John and Albert bought up half the town, but I bought my ranch and the livestock, and it cost every dime I had." He sighed. "Then Texas fever went through my herd. I lost all but seven of my cattle. All the money I'd carefully saved for my herd was gone. When William suggested I run against John for mayor, I knew the small amount it paid would help me to rebuild my herd, so I did it. That was twelve years ago. Every four years, John runs against me, and I always win."

Rosie smiled. "Good. I've met the man, and frankly, I didn't like him much. He seemed to look down on everyone around him. You're a good man, though. I knew it the moment I saw you."

Her words seemed to reach into him, lighting up his eyes with something warm and indefinable. "Thank you, Rosie," he murmured, "for seeing in me what I often forget."

The moment stretched between them, filled with an unspoken understanding, until the distant strains of fiddle music called them back to the present.

"Shall we dance, Mrs. Jordan?" Charles asked, extending his hand with a newfound tenderness.

"Lead the way, Mr. Jordan," Rosie replied, placing her hand in his.

As they moved together to join the dancers, their steps fell into rhythm with the spirited tune. The swirl of skirts, the stomp of boots, and the clapping hands surrounded them, but Rosie felt only the strength of Charles's arms guiding her and the harmony of their movements. With every turn and every step, the bond between them strengthened.

RAIN PATTERED AGAINST the windows of their cozy Hope Springs home, trapping Rosie and Charles indoors. Outside, the world was a blur of grey and green, but inside, they found warmth in the golden glow of lamplight and the rich scent of pine burning in the hearth.

"Your move, Mrs. Jordan," Charles announced with a mischievous glimmer in his eyes, gesturing toward the board game sprawled between them on the rug.

Rosie bit her lower lip in mock contemplation, her gaze flitting over the game pieces as if the fate of empires rested upon her decision. "I'm thinking," she teased, buying time to strategize her next play.

"Thinking or stalling?" Charles challenged, leaning closer under the pretense of scrutinizing the board. His arm brushed hers, sending an unbidden thrill through her.

"Stalling is a perfectly valid tactic," she countered. "Checkmate."

His jaw dropped, incredulity etched on his handsome face. "I'll be," he murmured, then leaned back with a hearty laugh that mingled with the thrumming of rain. "Looks like I've underestimated you once again."

Rosie's victory was sweetened when Charles reached out to tuck a stray curl behind her ear, his fingers lingering just a moment too long. Her heart skipped, and she caught her breath at the tenderness of the gesture. When his lips brushed her cheek, Rosie felt the barriers between them.

THE NEXT MORNING, WITH the skies cleared to a breathtaking azure, Charles led Rosie to the edge of the property where two horses waited, their coats gleaming in the sun. Rosie eyed the majestic creatures with a mix of awe and nervousness.

"Ever been riding before?" Charles asked, his voice laced with excitement.

"Only in my dreams," she admitted, her pulse quickening.

"Then today's the day your dream becomes reality." He offered her a hand, assisting her as she mounted the gentle gelding he'd chosen for her. "Take it slow, there's no rush."

She took a deep breath, feeling the strength of the horse between her legs, its muscles rippling with contained power. Charles swung onto his steed with practiced ease, tipping his hat back with a grin. "Ready?"

"Let's venture forth," she said, feeling that every day with Charles was an adventure.

They trotted into the mountains, leaving Hope Springs a fading patchwork of colors behind them. Rosie's initial trepidation gave way to exhilaration, her laughter mingling with the whisper of wind through the pines. Charles instructed her on posture and control, demonstrating with a patience she hadn't known he possessed.

"Like this?" Rosie asked, imitating his upright stance.

"Perfect," he praised, and she beamed under his approving gaze. "You're a natural."

"Feels like flying, doesn't it?" Charles called over the sound of hoofbeats on the mountain path.

"Better than flying," Rosie replied. "Of course, I've never flown, but I can imagine. I've had dreams of flying."

"Thank you, Charles," she said when they paused to take in the view, the valleys sprawling below them like a promise.

"For what?" he asked, dismounting to stand beside her.

"For teaching me to ride," she started, then smiled wider. "And for being the partner I never knew I needed."

Charles stepped closer, his hand finding hers, their fingers intertwining. "We're learning together, Rosie. That's the beauty of it."

The beauty indeed, Rosie thought, as Charles leaned in and their lips met in their first kiss. Above them, the sky stretched endlessly—a canvas awaiting the strokes of their unfolding love story.

THE WARMTH OF THE FIRE crackled, offsetting the chill that had settled over Hope Springs. Rosie nestled closer to Charles on the hearth-rug, a heavy blanket draped over their legs as they each held a well-worn book.

"Listen to this," Rosie said, her voice low and rich with enthusiasm, "'In her eyes, the glow of the soul's awakening shone.'" She looked up from the page, finding Charles's gaze already resting upon her with an intensity that made her heart flutter like the wings of a trapped sparrow.

"Such poetry in words," Charles replied. "But not nearly as captivating as the awakening I see when you speak of your dreams."

He cleared his throat, selecting a paragraph from his own book. As he read, Rosie couldn't help but marvel at the way his voice caressed the words, bringing the story to life with a passion that was both riveting and intimate.

When the clock tolled a late hour, Charles closed his book with a decisive snap. He glanced at the piano in the corner of the room—a silent invitation for yet another shared adventure.

"Have you ever played?" he asked, his eyebrow arching playfully as he extended a hand to help her up.

"Only in my dreams," she said, taking his hand and allowing him to lead her to the instrument.

"Then let dreams become reality tonight," Charles said, lifting the lid to reveal the ebony and ivory keys. Rosie watched, mesmerized, as his fingers began to dance across them, coaxing out a melody so tender it seemed to whisper secrets.

"Here, place your hands with mine," he instructed, guiding her to the keys. Their fingers brushed, a jolt of electricity passing between them, igniting a desire that was becoming increasingly difficult to ignore.

With gentle patience, Charles directed her through simple scales, their hands moving together in harmony. Rosie was a quick study, her laughter ringing out like a bell whenever she missed a note. But Charles never faltered, encouraging her with a smile that promised she'd soon be playing as if born to it.

"Like this," Charles murmured, their hands overlapping, his fingers deftly leading hers into the crescendo of the piece. The music swelled around them, filling the room with a beauty that seemed to pause time itself.

And in that suspended moment, as Rosie's hands moved under the guidance of Charles's, she knew that the magic of their connection was not confined to the notes they played or the words they read by firelight.

LATE ONE EVENING, ROSIE and Charles found themselves nestled in the heart of an overstuffed sofa, a fire crackling in the hearth. The evening's music lesson had drifted into silence, and in its place, a quiet anticipation hung between them.

"Charles," Rosie began, "have you ever imagined what legacy we'll leave here in Hope Springs?"

His eyes, usually so guarded, softened as he turned to face her. "I think about it often," he confessed. "More so now that you're here."

"Tell me," she urged, tucking a stray curl behind her ear.

He hesitated, but her encouraging smile coaxed his dreams out into the open. "I imagine a town where the feud is just a shadow of the past. A place thriving with trade and laughter, where every man, woman, and child feels they belong."

Rosie's heart swelled at his vision. "And a family?" she ventured, the word a soft tremor in the air.

"Yes, a family," Charles said, turning toward her with a tenderness that spoke volumes. "Children who know the value of community, who play in the meadows we once roamed...Our home, a sanctuary of love and growth."

Her hand found his. "It's a beautiful dream, Charles. One I share with all my heart."

"Rosie," Charles said, his voice barely above a whisper, "there are times when doubt creeps in, when I fear I'm not enough—for you, for this town."

"I have my fears too," she admitted, her breath warm against his skin. "Sometimes I worry I'll wake up and find that this is just a fleeting dream. And I'm back in Massachusetts, taking a beating because I refused to let my father hit my mother one more time."

"Then let's promise each other," Charles said, "to believe in our reality more than our fears."

"I promise," she whispered back.

CHARLES'S EYEBROWS rose in surprise as Rosie beckoned him toward the river, a wicker basket swinging from her arm.

"Rosie, what have you done?" he asked, as they rounded a bend and the secluded spot came into view.

"Consider it a respite from our duties," she replied with a sly smile, spreading a checkered blanket on the soft grass by the riverbank. "Even the mayor needs to eat."

The meal was simple fare, but every bite tasted of the care she had given to its preparation—a hearty stew, fresh bread, and apple pie, all followed by the rich aroma of strong coffee. They ate in companionable silence, occasionally exchanging looks that held more conversation than words ever could.

As the sunset painted the sky in strokes of pink and orange, they leaned back against an old oak. Charles's hand found hers, their fingers intertwining naturally. He turned to look at her, the fading light igniting flecks of amber in her eyes.

"Thank you for this," he whispered, his voice carrying the weight of unspoken gratitude for more than just the meal.

"Thank you for being here." Her response was immediate, punctuated by the gentle pressure of her hand squeezing his.

Their gazes locked, and for a moment, the world around them ceased to exist—their connection the only tangible thing. Then, they drew closer until their lips met in a kiss that was both an affirmation of their bond and a promise of more. It was passionate yet tender, filled with the yearning that had been simmering beneath the surface of their daily lives.

Breaking away, Rosie's laughter rang out, clear and joyous. "You should see your face, Mr. Mayor. All flushed with scandal."

"Scandal? In my Hope Springs?" Charles feigned shock, his eyes dancing with amusement. "I'll have you know I'm a very proper gentleman."

"Of course," Rosie teased, batting her eyelashes exaggeratedly. "As proper as they come, especially when whisking ladies away to secret picnics by the river."

"Only the most special of ladies," Charles said, his tone light but his intent serious. He brushed a stray lock of hair from her forehead, reveling in the simple act.

"Special, am I?" Rosie's voice was playful.

"You are," he said, leaning in so close his breath tickled her ear. "And I do believe you've bewitched me, Rosie Jordan."

"Is that so?" She tilted her head, her eyes alight with mischief. "Well then, Mr. Jordan, prepare to be thoroughly enchanted."

Chapter Five

Rosie's hand trembled as she reached up to brush a stray lock of hair from Charles's forehead. But there it was again—that flinch, subtle but undeniable. Charles withdrew from her touch as if he'd been scalded, his eyes a tumultuous sea of longing laced with unmistakable fear. For a man who commanded respect as the mayor, this vulnerability seemed out of place. She knew he'd been married before, so he had to have been touched by a woman. It was so strange to her.

"Goodnight, Rosie," he murmured.

"Goodnight, Charles," she replied, her voice a whisper lost in the shadows as she went to her bedroom. As she lay there, enveloped by the silence, her mind roared to life, teeming with doubts and questions that refused to be tamed.

What was it that caused him to recoil? Was it something within her that repelled him? The curve of her face, perhaps, or the way she laughed too loudly? Rosie turned onto her side, facing the large bay window where moonlight spilled through, painting silver streaks across the wooden floor.

Charles, the enigmatic man she had vowed to spend her life with, now felt like a stranger, his thoughts and desires hidden behind a wall she couldn't breach.

She pulled the quilt tighter around her shoulders, seeking comfort in its soft embrace—a poor substitute for the arms she longed to be held in. Was she not desirable? Her heart ached with the need to be seen, to be cherished. Hadn't she followed every unspoken rule of what a wife should be?

Rosie's brow furrowed as she battled the insecurities that nipped at her resolve. She was more than this, more than the doubts that crept into her heart like unwelcome guests. And she was determined, come morning, to find a bridge across the divide that had settled between them, to ignite a spark that would illuminate both their hearts with the fire of true companionship.

For now, though, the night stretched on, a silent witness to Rosie's vigil, her thoughts a carousel of worry and wonder, spinning tirelessly until dawn's light would bring with it new possibilities.

AT BREAKFAST THE NEXT morning, Rosie watched Charles as he buttered his toast. She took in his features and felt a familiar ache in her chest.

"Charles?" she asked, her voice soft but steady. "May I speak with you about something important?"

He glanced up from his plate, his blue eyes meeting hers briefly before skirting away. "Of course, Rosie," he said, a guarded note in his voice. "What's on your mind?"

She reached across the table, her fingers hovering just shy of his hand—a touch she yearned to give and receive freely. "It's us," she confessed. "I feel like there's a distance between us, and I don't know what to do to get closer. You pull away from me after you've seemed so close for a while. I want to fix it!"

Charles set down his knife with a clink, schooling his expression. "Everything is fine, my dear," he replied. "Marriage is...well, it's an adjustment for both of us."

Rosie bit her lip, her intuition telling her there was more to it than he was admitting. She pushed forward, determined to get to the bottom of things.

"An adjustment, yes," she agreed gently, "but one I hoped we'd work on together. I want to understand you, Charles, all of you—even the parts that might be difficult to share."

His gaze flickered to hers again, a storm brewing in his eyes before he shuttered them away behind polite indifference. "I appreciate your concern, Rosie," he said, "but everything's all right. We're doing quite well, considering."

"Considering?" Rosie echoed. She wouldn't let this be the end of it, not when her heart told her there was so much more to their story than the chapters they were pretending to live.

"Yes, considering," Charles repeated, his voice firmer now, though she could hear the undercurrent of something raw and unspoken.

Rosie nodded, accepting his answer for the moment while knowing this was only the beginning of their journey. They would figure it out together.

For now, she simply smiled and offered him a refill on his drink. "More coffee?"

Charles accepted the coffee with a nod. As discouraged as Rosie got at times, she was optimistic about her future. And even if she wasn't, she'd stay in Hope Springs, if only to be close to her sisters.

ROSIE WATCHED CHARLES. He stood by the window, his back to her, gazing outside. The view offered comfort and space for reflection, and yet Rosie knew it was not the beauty of the sunset that held him captive. It was something that happened to him in the past, and she would love to be able to understand why he vacillated between loving husband and stranger.

"Charles?" Her voice was soft. "Talk to me."

He turned slightly. "Rosie," he began, his voice carrying a weariness that spoke of battles fought in silence, "I don't want to burden you with my troubles."

"Burden?" She stepped closer, bridging the gap between them with a courage she didn't know she possessed. "I married you wanting all of your tomorrows, but I can't ignore your yesterdays if they're holding you back from me."

"Rosie, I..." He trailed off, his gaze dropping to where his hands were braced against the windowsill.

She reached out, placing her hand atop his, feeling the tremor that ran through him. "We're in this together."

Charles turned fully, the last rays of the sun catching the hint of moisture in his eyes. "My late wife..." The words came reluctantly, each one pulled from a well of pain. "She had this way of making me feel like I wasn't enough. My ideas, my desires...they were all under her thumb, twisted until I barely recognized myself."

Rosie's heart clenched at the confession, her resolve strengthening. "But you're not that man anymore, Charles. You're the mayor, respected by all, and you're my husband." Her smile was tinged with empathy.

"Rosie, I'm afraid." His voice cracked. "Afraid that if I let myself be vulnerable again, I'll lose myself once more."

She squeezed his hand. "We'll ride through every storm, and I'll be right here, holding on tight, never letting go."

A small chuckle escaped Charles, a sound so rare and precious that Rosie felt a flicker of triumph. There was humor there, a glimmer of light amidst the darkness, and she knew they had taken another step toward healing.

"Thank you, Rosie," he said, finally meeting her eyes. "For seeing me, for hearing me...and for not making me feel like I'm less a man in your eyes."

"Always," she promised, her voice steady and sure.

ROSIE LACED HER BOOTS. Today she had planned a picnic by the river, and not even the brooding Colorado skies could dampen her spirits. The air was crisp—alive with the scent of pine and the promise of rain—as she stepped out onto the wooden porch of their modest home.

"Ready to test your fishing skills, Mr. Mayor?" Rosie called back through the open door.

Charles appeared in the doorway, a smile tugging at his lips. "Only if you're prepared to witness the master at work," he replied.

They walked side by side down the path that wound its way toward the river, shoulders occasionally brushing, an electric current of unspoken understanding passing between them. As they settled on the grassy bank, Rosie unpacked the basket, laying out sandwiches and fresh-baked apple pie, while Charles tackled the fishing line with clumsy enthusiasm.

"Remember, it's all in the wrist," Rosie advised. She and her sisters had spent many afternoons sneaking down to the creek near their parents' farm and fishing. They'd never been able to eat their catch because their father would have "punished" them and their mother if he'd found out, but that hadn't stopped the three sisters' enjoyment of their outings.

"Ah, I'm lulling the fish into a false sense of security," Charles retorted, casting again with slightly more success.

It was during these shared meals, these gentle teases, that Rosie found herself falling deeper for the man. And she could tell by the ease in Charles's posture, the warmth in his gaze, that he too was succumbing to feelings for her.

As the afternoon waned, they strolled along the river, speaking of dreams and the future. Rosie spoke of her love for literature, and to her delight, Charles confessed his fondness for poetry, reciting lines from memory with a passion that made her heart swell.

"Byron's words always stirred something within me," Charles admitted. "Though I never had much use for them in politics."

"Then we shall have poetry nights," Rosie declared. "Just you, me, and the beauty of the spoken word."

The idea sparked a new connection, a shared realm where they could both be vulnerable yet emboldened by each other's presence. With every step, every shared secret and whispered dreams.

As dusk embraced the world in its indigo shawl, they reluctantly packed their belongings and headed home.

ROSIE WATCHED AS CHARLES meticulously tended to the small herb garden at the back of their homestead. The delicate way his fingers worked through the soil, a tenderness in his touch that she'd longed to feel against her own skin, was a dance of shadow and sunlight that played across his features. She leaned against the wooden doorframe, a smile tugging at the corners of her lips. The man before her was blossoming.

"Your basil seems to be thriving," Rosie remarked.

"Ah, but it's the thyme that truly prospers under careful watch," Charles replied.

"Time and patience," Rosie mused aloud.

"Yes." He stood and dusted off his hands, walking toward her. "And speaking of time, I believe it's high time for that poetry night you proposed."

Rosie smiled and nodded. "I think that's a great idea.

They settled in the parlor. A few candles flickered, casting a soft glow on the pages of the book that lay open on Rosie's lap. Her voice rose and fell with the rhythm of the poems, each word a note in a symphony that filled the room and wound its way around Charles's heart.

As she read, Charles watched her, thinking of how long it had been since he'd held a woman.

"Your voice gives life to these verses," Charles said softly when she paused.

"Only because the sentiment behind them is one I share," Rosie replied, her gaze locking with his.

They were close enough to feel each other's breath. Yet, they did not cross the invisible line that held them apart, the physical boundary that remained unchallenged for now.

"Thank you, Rosie," Charles said. "For your patience...for everything."

"Thank you, Charles," Rosie said, "for letting me see you."

Their fingers brushed as they closed the book together, a fleeting caress that left Rosie's heart aflutter with unresolved yearnings. But beneath the tumult of her emotions was a steady flame of hope, rekindled by the man before her—a man who was learning to love again.

Chapter Six

Rosie perched on the edge of their sofa, a quilt wrapped around her shoulders as she watched Charles stoke the fireplace. It was a simple evening in Hope Springs, the kind that seemed to wrap the town in an embrace of tranquility.

"Got that fire roaring like a dragon's breath," Rosie said, her eyes twinkling with mischief.

Charles glanced over his shoulder, the corners of his mouth inching up into a smile. "Only the best for my lady," he said, playing along with the light-hearted. "Wouldn't want you catching a cold now, would we?"

"Of course not, Mr. Jordan. The mayor and his wife must maintain a picture of health, after all," Rosie teased.

Charles took a seat beside her, the sofa creaking under his weight. He spoke of his day, recounting the minor victories and the mundane setbacks with equal measure, always careful to elicit a laugh from Rosie when the tales grew too dull.

"And what of your day, Mrs. Jordan?" he inquired, turning toward her with genuine interest.

"Ah, well," Rosie started, tucking a strand of hair behind her ear, "I had quite the adventure arguing with Mrs. Peabody over the price of eggs—felt like negotiating a peace treaty."

"Mrs. Peabody does drive a hard bargain," Charles chuckled, his eyes crinkling at the edges. "But I have no doubt you held your ground."

"Of course," she replied, her head held high with feigned haughtiness before dissolving into laughter.

ROSIE AWOKE WITH A purpose, slipping outside to gather eggs and then going into the kitchen to make a special breakfast for Charles. Maybe he wasn't willing to accept her love just yet, but he sure didn't mind eating the meals she made.

Her fingers danced across the countertop as she gathered ingredients. Flour puffed into the air as she kneaded dough, her cheeks dusted with white. Eggs sizzled in the skillet, and the aroma of freshly brewed coffee began to fill the room. She hummed a tune under her breath, a melody that spoke of hope and new beginnings.

Rosie wanted to create something special, a breakfast that would not only satiate hunger but also convey the affection she held for Charles—a silent language of love spoken through buttery pastries and perfectly scrambled eggs. With each whisk and stir, she poured her heart into the meal, hoping it would bridge the gap between them, inching closer to the warmth she longed for in Charles's embrace.

Rosie set the table with delicate care, arranging the dishes perfectly. She stepped back to admire her handiwork, a spread worthy of royalty, or at least the mayor of Hope Springs.

Charles paused on the threshold of the kitchen, the aroma of Rosie's cooking tugging at him like a warm embrace. The sight that greeted him was one he would not soon forget: the table bathed in the morning light, set with a care that spoke volumes of her quiet dedication. Plates piled high with fluffy pancakes and golden eggs beckoned invitingly, each dish a testament to her desire to please.

"Rosie," he said, his voice laced with an emotion he seldom showed, "this is...extraordinary." He moved across the room, the wooden floorboards creaking beneath his boots.

Her smile flickered. "I hoped you'd like it," she said, her heart skipping a beat as she caught the genuine appreciation in his eyes. For a moment, they were not just mayor and wife, but two souls reaching across the chasm of unspoken words.

"Like it?" Charles chuckled, pulling out a chair with more gusto than usual. "I believe 'like' is too meager a word for this feast."

They ate, and with each shared glance, Rosie felt a little more of the frost around them thaw.

"Charles, we need to talk about Hope Springs. Troubles are brewing that can't be ignored any longer."

He nodded, setting down his cup with a decisive click. "I've felt it, too. The Wilson's farm is struggling since the drought, and Miss Baker's schoolhouse is in dire need of repair."

"Then there's Doctor Mercer who needs help with the infirmary supplies," Rosie added, her mind racing with the urgency of their town's needs.

"Yes," Charles agreed. "We need to support them. It will help the entire community."

"Perhaps..." Rosie said, hesitating only a moment before conviction bolstered her resolve. "Perhaps we could start a fund, something that everyone can contribute to according to their means. A collective effort."

"Ah, Rosie, I so admire your spirit," Charles said. "You see the heart of the matter and aren't afraid to tackle it head-on."

"Someone has to," she replied.

"Let's pool our ideas together. We'll draft a plan after breakfast," Charles declared, rolling up his sleeves. "For Hope Springs, for us—"

"—For our future," Rosie finished, warmth flooding her cheeks. Together, they set about solving the problems of their little world. And as they talked, the distance between them seemed less insurmountable with each passing word.

ROSIE PENNED A LIST with meticulous care, her brows knitting in concentration. A stack of flyers sat ready on the table, each beckoning the residents of Hope Springs to their civic duty. She had taken charge of the organizational aspects of the town meeting, a responsibility that fit her like a glove.

"Already hard at work, I see," Charles remarked, entering the room with a sense of purpose that matched the early hour. The corners of his mouth lifted in appreciation as he observed the tidy space Rosie had transformed into a room for community planning.

"Good morning, Charles," Rosie greeted him. "I've outlined the agenda and drafted a flyer. We'll need to get these posted everywhere—by the general store, the saloon, the church..."

"Leave it to me," Charles assured her. He understood the importance of getting every soul in Hope Springs involved. "I'll make certain everyone knows about the meeting and feels welcome to attend. "

"Thank you," she said, biting her lip thoughtfully. "It means a lot to have your support in this. Not just as the mayor, but...as my husband."

A spark of something unspoken passed between them, a shared understanding that they were embarking on a journey bigger than themselves. With that, Charles set out, leaving Rosie to finalize the details of their ambitious endeavor.

ROSIE AND CHARLES REACHED the town hall well before anyone else. They'd decided to have the meeting on Sunday afternoon, so they would be assured most people wouldn't be working. Together, they arranged chairs into neat rows, spreading tablecloths and setting out pitchers of water for the townspeople.

"Looks inviting, doesn't it?" Charles mused, overseeing the preparations with a hint of pride. His usual reserve seemed to melt away in the face of communal spirit.

"Inviting and hopeful," Rosie said. "Let's hope the townsfolk agree." Rosie placed the last chair down with a satisfying clunk. The room was ready.

"Agreed," Charles said, extending his hand to Rosie. "Together, let's lead them into a new chapter."

Rosie stood at the front of the crowded room, her hands resting lightly on the makeshift podium. "Thank you all for coming," Rosie began, her voice steady as the gazebo in the town square. "We're here to discuss the problems facing our town and what we can do to solve them."

Nods and murmurs of agreement fluttered through the crowd. Charles stood just off to the side, watching the townspeople. Each time Rosie glanced his way, she drew strength from his silent encouragement. He was her rock, even if at times he felt more like a mystery.

"Jed, why don't you start us off?" Rosie nodded toward an elder. Jed stood, his voice gruff.

"Water rights," he declared, and like a spark to tinder, the room ignited.

"Land boundaries!" another shouted.

"Schooling for our children!" came a call from the back.

"Enough!" Rosie said, her tone brooking no argument. Silence fell.

"Let's tackle these one at a time," Rosie proposed, her fingers brushing against a list she'd prepared. As she spoke, she shared glances with Charles. They were partners, in this endeavor if nothing else.

Charles stepped forward when talk turned to land disputes, his knowledge of local laws surfacing with ease. Rosie watched him mediate between two quarreling ranchers. She saw the respect in the townsfolks' eyes, and pride swelled within her.

"Perhaps we could survey the lands again, together," Charles suggested. The men nodded reluctantly.

"Surveying's fine," a wiry woman piped up, "but what about our children's learning? My Billy can't read!"

"Valid point, Mrs. Dalton." Rosie's response was swift. "Education is the foundation upon which we build our future. Let's discuss how we might bolster our efforts there."

Ideas volleyed back and forth. When tensions flared over whether to prioritize new schoolbooks or repairs to the town hall, Rosie stood firm.

"Friends," she implored, "let's remember that our goals are the same, even if our paths diverge. We *all* seek prosperity and happiness for Hope Springs, do we not?"

Heads bobbed in agreement. Charles offered solutions, his quiet strength complementing Rosie's fiery passion.

As the meeting drew to a close, Rosie felt the weight of responsibility on her shoulders lighten.

"Thank you, everyone," she said, her heart full. "Together, we've taken a step toward unity and understanding. Let's continue this journey with open hearts and minds."

"Here, here!" the room echoed, and as Rosie looked out over the faces before her, she knew they had achieved something significant.

Rosie's eyes sparkled with the fire of inspiration. "Our plan," she began, "will lay the foundation for a Hope Springs that our children, and their children after them, can take pride in."

Rosie explained the plan for their future. Her words painted the picture of a revitalized main street, better education, and ways to settle land and water disputes.

"Healthcare," Charles interjected, his steady tone a harmonious counterpoint to Rosie's ardent pitch, "is paramount. No man, woman, or child should lie awake at night, fearing illness because help is beyond reach." Nods of agreement rippled through the crowd as he detailed plans to expand the local clinic.

"And education," Rosie continued, the light of determination in her gaze, "will be our beacon, guiding us toward enlightenment and prosperity." She spoke of new textbooks, of teachers sharing knowledge under roofs that didn't leak and walls that promised sanctuary from the harsh mountain winds.

A short while later, Rosie and Charles found themselves alone amid the rows of empty chairs. Charles reached for Rosie's hand. "We've sown seeds of change today," he said.

"I think we have," Rosie replied, a faint tremor betraying the emotion she worked to keep at bay. "But a seed must weather many storms before it blooms."

"Hope Springs will flourish," Charles stated, conviction bolstering his stance. "Because we will toil and dream and fight for it—together."

Rosie's heart thrummed, the promise in his words igniting a flame within. "Together," she echoed, allowing herself to lean ever so slightly into his strength.

As they walked home in silence, Rosie contemplated the past few hours. The meeting had been a triumph, and it felt good to have a plan of action.

Rosie made a quick supper, and while they ate, she told him a story about something that had happened while she'd been with Izzy and Ana.

"Ana's face was the very picture of bewilderment," Rosie said, her voice dancing with mirth as she shed her outerwear and moved closer to the fire. "One moment she's sitting with Izzy and I in the parlor, the next—she finds a baby swaddled on her doorstep!"

Charles watched her, smiling as he watched her animated gestures. It was these unguarded moments, when Rosie's vivacity shone, that he found himself drawn to her most. "A baby?" he echoed, amusement flickering across his features.

"Yes!" Rosie's laughter tinkled through the room, as bright and clear as the stars they'd left behind. "She scooped that child up as if it were the most natural thing, cooing to it as though it were a stray kitten rather than a babe of unknown origin. Not that I think she would have been any different if she had known the origin. I do believe they'll keep her."

His chuckle mingled with hers, low and rich. He stepped forward, drawn by the infectious joy in her eyes, and encircled her waist with his arms, pulling her close. Their bodies met—a fitting puzzle of angles and curves—and for a suspended heartbeat, Rosie's laughter ceased, her breath catching in anticipation.

"Rosie," Charles murmured. His fingers traced the line of her jaw, tilting her face up to meet his gaze. In the depths of his eyes, she glimpsed the burgeoning flame of desire.

"Charles," she whispered back. There was no need for more.

He kissed her then. His lips were warm, insistent, and she wrapped her arms around him, pressing herself against the man she was beginning to love.

When they finally parted, breathless and flushed, Rosie rested her head against his chest, listening to the steady rhythm of his heart.

"Let us not tell Ana her doorstep intruder has become tonight's anecdote," Charles said.

"Agreed," Rosie responded, her voice soft against his shirtfront. "Some tales are best kept between partners."

Rosie and Charles stood wrapped in each other's embrace, the space between them filled with laughter, hope, and the whisper of something more.

Rosie's heart raced as Charles's strong hands traced the delicate curve of her waist, pulling her closer. Their breaths mingled, warm and tentative.

Rosie lifted her gaze to meet his, finding oceans of unspoken promises in his eyes.

"Charles, I've never..." she said, blushing.

"I know, darling," he said, a smile touching the corners of his mouth, softening the serious set of his jaw.

"Then let's discover this...together," Rosie whispered, her fingers tentatively exploring the buttons of his vest, undoing them one by one with an innocent boldness. Finally, they were going to have a real marriage, and Rosie couldn't be happier about it.

A chuckle escaped Charles as he assisted her fumbling fingers. "Together," he said, his hands now mirroring hers, working the fastenings at the back of her dress with deft movements that spoke of a man who knew the value of patience and care.

Rosie shivered, not from cold but from the thrill of intimacy, the heat of Charles's gaze igniting fires of longing that had lain dormant within her soul.

"Are you certain?" Charles asked, his voice husky, his hands poised at the final barrier to her modesty.

"More than I've ever been," she replied.

But soon, each touch, each whisper, each breath they shared bound them not just in duty to their town but to each other.

As Rosie surrendered to the sensations that Charles's cautious, caring hands evoked, the world outside faded.

With the night enshrouding them in its velvet embrace, they explored each other.

Afterward, Rosie's head rested on Charles's chest, his heartbeat a steady drum lulling her into a serenity she'd never known.

The heat of the night still lingered on their skin. Charles's arms were around her. She finally felt like a married woman. His fingers traced idle patterns along her back, soothing the remnants of a passion that had both undone and remade her.

As sleep beckoned, Rosie felt the light tug of tomorrow's worries, yet they seemed distant, muted by the profound shift in her heart. There, in the sanctuary of Charles's embrace, she found hope, not just for Hope Springs, but for the life they were building together, stitch by passionate stitch.

And as slumber finally claimed them, the promise of dawn waited patiently, a quiet guardian to their dreams. For tomorrow would bring its challenges, yes, but also its joys.

Chapter Seven

Rosie slid the eggs onto the plate with less care than usual, her mind elsewhere. Charles sat across from her, his usually expressive eyes hidden behind the high wall of his coffee cup, which he clung to as if it were a shield.

"Did you sleep well?" she ventured, trying to inject some normalcy into the strained silence.

"Fine," Charles grunted without looking up.

Rosie chewed on a piece of toast, feeling the rough texture against her tongue but tasting nothing. It was their first breakfast together after sharing a night of unexpected closeness. But now, with the light of day filtering through the lace curtains, that awkwardness, and it was much worse than before.

She reached for the jam, the clink of her knife against the jar a sharp note in the quiet room. Charles seemed lost in his own world, his gaze fixed firmly on the grain of the wooden table.

"Anything on your agenda today?" Rosie tried again.

"Work," was all he said, and with a last sip of coffee, he rose, excusing himself with a mumbled need to see to some ranch duties.

Left alone with the remnants of breakfast, Rosie knew she needed air. She went to the hardware store, determined to use her energy for something productive.

The bell above the shop door announced her entry. Mr. Jenkins, the proprietor, peered at her from behind wire-rimmed spectacles, his eyes crinkling with a smile that was as much a part of the store as the shelves of nails and bins of bolts.

"Good morning, Rosie!" he called out. "What brings you in today?"

"Good morning, Mr. Jenkins," Rosie replied. "I'm looking for information on pumps and pipes. We're planning some improvements around town."

"Ah, infrastructure!" Mr. Jenkins exclaimed, rubbing his hands together. "Well, you've come to the right place. Follow me, let's see what we can rustle up for you."

As they walked through the aisles, Mr. Jenkins shared tales of past projects and offered advice on the best materials for durability in the harsh Colorado winters. Rosie listened intently, her notebook filling with sketches and notes, the weight of the morning's unease lifting slightly.

"Thank you, Mr. Jenkins. I truly appreciate your help," Rosie replied, her cheeks warming with gratitude.

"Anytime, my dear. Oh, and Rosie?" he added, a twinkle in his eye. "Don't let the men folk get you down. You've got more gumption than most of 'em put together."

Rosie laughed. As she stepped out of the store, carrying a catalog she could order from, she felt a renewed sense of purpose. Yes, there were challenges ahead, both in her work for the town and in her marriage to Charles, but Rosie had always been one to face obstacles head-on. And she had the scars to prove it.

With a spring in her step, she made her way to Ana's house. Some time with her sisters and Lillian was exactly what she needed.

ROSIE SETTLED INTO the plush sofa in Ana's parlor, her gaze lingering on baby Lillian who was cooing contentedly in her cradle. The warmth of the hearth fought off the chill from the Colorado winter outside, and Rosie felt a flicker of an idea that could bring that same warmth to the entire town.

"Ana, Izzy," Rosie began, her enthusiasm bubbling over as she leaned forward. "What if we organized a Christmas fair? It'd be grand, with decorations and stalls for local artisans. We could raise money for the repairs that the town desperately needs."

Ana rocked gently in her chair, knitting needles clicking rhythmically. "A fair?" she mused, a smile tugging at the corners of her lips. "That does sound like fun."

Izzy giggled. "And you know how folks around here love a good celebration. It could be the perfect way to spread some cheer and fill up the town's coffers. And I'd be willing to bet Albert would like to show his paintings off and maybe even sell a few."

Rosie nodded, her mind already racing with plans. "We could have it all - garlands, music, even a tree lighting ceremony!" Her voice lifted with excitement, and even baby Lillian seemed to sense the infectious optimism, her little hands reaching out as if applauding the idea.

Ana set down her knitting, her eyes alight with the vision. "It's ambitious, Rosie, but if anyone can make it happen, it's you." Her endorsement warmed Rosie's heart, bolstering her resolve.

Meanwhile, across town, Charles Jordan stood before the gathering of Hope Springs' most influential men.

"Gentlemen," Charles intoned. "Our town stands poised on the brink of change. The initiatives we put forth today will carve the path for our future prosperity."

He unfurled a map across the table, his fingers tracing the lines where new roads would go, where wells could provide fresh water, where the schoolhouse needed expansion.

"Consider this," he continued, locking eyes with each council member in turn. "An investment in our infrastructure is an investment in ourselves—our children, our businesses, our legacy."

Murmurs of agreement rippled through the room. A councilman stroked his beard thoughtfully, nodding along to Charles's impassioned pitch.

"Furthermore," Charles said, "the success of these projects hinges on community involvement. We'll need every pair of willing hands, every ounce of local pride to see this through."

The room echoed with the claps of approval, the men rallying behind their mayor's vision—a testament to Charles's ability to unite them under a common cause.

ROSIE FORKED A SLICE of ham, her appetite waning in the thick silence that cloaked the dinner table like an unwelcome winter fog. Charles sat opposite her; his gaze locked on his plate as if the mashed potatoes might reveal life's greatest mysteries. The air was heavy with words unsaid, and Rosie's heart drummed a nervous rhythm against her chest.

"Charles," she said, "I've been thinking about how to bring some cheer to Hope Springs this Christmas."

He looked up then, eyes clouded with something like apprehension. "Go on," he said, his voice steady but distant.

"Imagine a Christmas fair right here in town," Rosie said, the words tumbling out. "We could have booths for local craftsmen and people to sell their handmade goods. It would be a chance for them to showcase their talents and for us to raise the necessary funds. Izzy is almost certain Albert will want a booth."

Her hands gestured animatedly, painting the scene in the air between them. "And what about a snowman contest for the children?" she added, her cheeks flushed with the warmth of her vision. "It would be such fun, don't you think?"

Charles nodded slowly, a thoughtful crease forming between his brows. "Food," he suggested after a moment. "Every good gathering needs sustenance. Warm soups, freshly baked bread, pies that remind you of home."

"A splendid idea!" Rosie exclaimed. Her heart fluttered with hope, seeing the hint of a smile playing at the corner of his lips.

The meal concluded with a few more exchanges about logistics and dates, the clinking of cutlery serving as a gentle underscore to their collaborative planning. But as the last bite was taken and the final crumbs brushed away, an invisible barrier seemed to rise once again.

"Shall we retire?" Charles asked, his chair scraping back with a finality that echoed ominously in Rosie's ears.

"Of course," she replied, her voice a soft feather in the suddenly cavernous dining room.

As they stood, Charles turned to her. "I'll see you in the morning," he said simply, his voice devoid of the day's earlier warmth.

"Goodnight, then," Rosie murmured, her heart sinking into the pit of her stomach. She watched him retreat and understood with crushing clarity that he had put his heart and bed out of her reach.

Rosie ascended the stairs alone. She reached the top and paused, glancing toward the closed door of Charles's room, feeling the finality of his words as keenly as the chill from the frosted windows.

With a deep breath, she turned away, her door closing softly behind her. The room felt colder than usual, and Rosie wrapped her arms around herself, seeking comfort.

Rosie sat on the edge of her bed, the silence of the room amplifying the turmoil within her. Her hands clutched at the quilt she and her sisters had made, seeking solace in its familiar texture. What could have turned the tide of Charles's affections so swiftly? She replayed the evening's conversation in her mind, searching for a misstep, an errant word that might have caused this rift.

She leaned back, the soft pillow catching her as she gazed at the ceiling. Tears welled in her eyes, trickling down her cheeks. She wiped them away with a lace handkerchief, chastising herself for allowing hope to grow. With each shuddering breath, she willed sleep to come and bring respite from her thoughts.

PAPERS WERE STREWN across the table where Rosie and Charles now sat. They were surrounded by ledgers and maps of Hope Springs.

"Here," Rosie said, pointing to a section of the map, "we can build the new well. It'll serve the west side of town where they've been struggling with water access."

"Agreed," Charles replied. "And we'll need to set a deadline for two months from now. I'll speak with the blacksmith about forging the necessary components."

"Excellent." Rosie's eyes sparkled with determination. "We can allocate some of the funds raised from the Christmas fair for materials, and perhaps Mr. Jenkins's carpentry skills will be useful for the housing."

Charles looked up, meeting her gaze for the first time since they'd spent a night together. "You're quite adept at this, Rosie."

Rosie blushed but held his gaze. "It takes two, Charles. We're a team, after all."

"We are," Charles conceded, a half-smile tugging at the corner of his mouth. The tone was businesslike, but there was a warmth there that had been absent of late.

"Your organizational skills are impressive," Charles noted, jotting down another of Rosie's ideas. "You bring new life and enthusiasm to everything around you."

"Thank you," she replied. "We'll need enthusiasm to get things done."

"True enough," he chuckled, and for a moment, the room seemed lighter.

As they continued working, a comfortable rhythm established itself between them. Each task was met with thoughtful discussion.

For now, Rosie focused on the plans before them. And as the hours passed, she believed someday he would return her love. She'd always been an optimist, and she thought it was her best quality. Why not make certain she used it when she needed it?

Rosie leaned back in her chair, stretching the stiffness from her spine, seeking Charles's eyes for a shared moment of respite.

"Quite a day," she ventured with an easy smile, hoping to bridge the gap between them. "Mr. Jenkins is on board with the new water pump design, and says it'll change the town for the better."

"Good, good..." Charles murmured. Rosie's smile wavered, the familiar pang of confusion pricking at her heart. They were a team in every sense, yet he kept her at arm's length.

"Charles?" she prodded gently, reaching across the table to touch his hand. His fingers were cool under hers, and he looked up, almost startled by the contact.

"Rosie," he started, "I'm...sorry." He withdrew his hand subtly, erecting his walls once more. "It's just—the mill expansion, the school supplies, the winter stores—there's much to consider."

"Of course," Rosie said, pulling her hand back and folding it in her lap. Her concern deepened at his evasion.

"Talk to me, Charles," she urged, her voice soft but insistent. "I see you, lost in thought far too often. It's more than just the town's troubles, isn't it?"

"Rosie, I assure you," he said with a measured calm, "my preoccupation is with our work. There's nothing to worry about."

She nodded, though unconvinced, her intuition whispering that there was a depth to Charles's distraction that went unsaid. Rosie pushed a stray curl behind her ear and decided to let the matter rest—for now. With a determined tilt to her chin, she refocused her attention on the ledger.

"All right, then," she declared, her tone laced with a hopeful buoyancy. "Let's tackle this one step at a time. Together."

Her words hung in the air. Yet as the evening wore on, and they delved back into discussions of budget allocations and deadlines, Rosie couldn't shake the feeling that Charles was miles away. And so she resolved to wait. She knew they'd find their way eventually.

ROSIE'S HEART SWELLED as she watched the children of Hope Springs frolic on the playground, their laughter music to her ears. Standing beside Charles at the edge of the land they had worked so hard to give to the school, she felt a warmth that had little to do with the afternoon sun and everything to do with the shared triumph lighting up his eyes.

"Look at them, Charles," she said. "It's like we've given them a new language—a language of joy."

Charles nodded. "They deserve every bit of happiness we can give them."

The townspeople, one by one, approached with words of gratitude. Old man Watson, who owned the general store, tipped his hat to them both. "This here playground is going to change things for the better. You mark my words."

"Thank you, Mr. Watson," Rosie replied, her cheeks flushed from more than just the crisp Colorado air. "We couldn't have done it without everyone's support."

"Nor without each other," Charles added softly.

Rosie's heart skipped at the possibility that maybe, just maybe, they were on the brink of reconnecting on a level deeper than before.

Later that week, after a particularly grueling session with the town council, Charles surprised Rosie by suggesting they take a break from the relentless pace.

"Let's go for a sleigh ride," he suggested.

"Really?" Her response was incredulous but hopeful. "But there's still so much to do—"

"Exactly why we need a respite. To remember why we're doing all this." His voice was firm but gentle.

Bundled against the cold, they set off through the streets, the clop-clop of the horse's hooves syncing with the racing of Rosie's heart. The world around them was a white canvas, untouched and serene.

"Isn't it beautiful?" she murmured, her breath visible in the wintry air.

"Yes," Charles agreed, though his gaze remained fixed on her rather than the scenery. "It reminds me of you—how you've brought beauty and life to my world."

Rosie turned to him, startled by the intensity behind his words. A blush crept over her cheeks even as a thrill ran down her spine.

"Charles, I—"

"Shh," he interrupted with a finger to her lips. "No need for words. Not now."

For the rest of the ride, they sat in comfortable silence, each lost in thoughts that were perhaps not as distant from the other's as they might have imagined. The sleigh glided over the snow, past the church, the schoolhouse, and homes adorned with wreaths and ribbons.

And when the sleigh slowed to a stop back at their home, Charles offered his hand to help Rosie down, his touch lingering longer than necessary. She looked up at him, her eyes searching for that elusive connection.

"Thank you, Charles," she said. "For this, for everything."

"Rosie," he began, then hesitated. Whatever words he sought seemed to elude him, but the emotion in his eyes spoke volumes.

"Come inside," she urged gently, leading him by the hand. "It's getting cold."

Charles shook his head. "I need to take care of the horses."

Rosie felt a flicker of hope that the walls Charles had built around himself might melt away.

ROSIE PACED THE LENGTH of Ana's parlor, the hem of her skirt whispering secrets against the polished wooden floor. Baby Lillian slumbered in a cradle by the hearth, her tiny fists curled like delicate seashells.

"Ana," Rosie began, halting mid-stride. "I need to talk to you about Charles."

Ana set aside her embroidery and gave her sister an encouraging nod. "What's troubling you?"

Rosie sighed. "It's just that...I can't shake the feeling that something is weighing on him. He's here but not here, if you understand my meaning."

"Charles carries more than his share of burdens," Ana said softly. "He's the mayor, after all. The whole town looks to him."

"I know that, and I admire his dedication," Rosie replied, brushing a lock of hair from her face. "But it's more personal, I think. There's a distance in his eyes... Perhaps you could ask William about him. I feel it all has to do with his first wife, but I simply don't know *how*."

"Rosie, dear." Ana stood and took Rosie's hands in hers. "You must be patient with him. Men like Charles—they're not so different from us. They need time to heal from the droughts and storms life throws their way. Give him time. If he hasn't come around by Christmas, I'll talk to William about him."

"Patience has never been my strong suit," Rosie admitted with a rueful chuckle, finding solace in the familiar cadence of her sister's wisdom.

"Then consider this another challenge for you to conquer," Ana said with a twinkle in her eye. "Keep showing him your support, your love. Don't press for confessions or revelations. When Charles is ready, he'll open up. And until then, your unwavering presence will be the balm his heart needs, whether he knows it or not."

Rosie nodded, drawing strength from Ana's words. "I shall stand by him."

"That's the spirit." Ana squeezed Rosie's hands before releasing them. "And remember, sometimes the most profound changes happen slowly and quietly and not all at once."

"Thank you, Ana," Rosie whispered, a sense of resolve kindling within her.

ROSIE WRAPPED HER SHAWL tighter around her shoulders, feeling the comforting weight of Ana's advice settle within her.

She would be patient with Charles; she would give him the time he needed to come to terms with whatever inner turmoil kept him at arm's length. Her love for him was as wide and deep as the valley they called home, and she trusted it to carry them through any storm.

As Rosie walked toward the general store, she envisioned their future like one of the majestic pines surrounding their town—reaching for the sky against all odds. Laughter bubbled up from within her as she imagined herself and Charles, many years from now, standing side by side like two old trees with intertwined roots.

"Morning, Mrs. Jordan!" greeted Mr. Whitaker, the postman, tipping his hat as he passed her on the street.

"Good morning, Mr. Whitaker," Rosie replied with a smile, her heart lightening at the simple exchange. This community had become hers, and Charles was at the center of it—a center she was determined to hold onto.

As she entered the store, the bell above the door jangled cheerfully, announcing her presence. She moved with purpose, making a list of what they needed for the upcoming Christmas fair. She could already hear the laughter of children building snowmen and the chatter of townsfolk admiring the local crafts. It was a vision she and Charles would bring to life together.

"Mrs. Jordan, you're looking mighty determined today," observed Mr. Watson, the store owner, as he approached with a friendly nod.

" I am, Mr. Watson. We've got a fair to prepare for, and I intend to make it the finest this town has ever seen," Rosie declared, her eyes sparkling with mirth.

"Ah, that's the spirit we need," he chuckled, leaning on the counter. "Say, how's the mayor holding up? I know this is a lot with him trying to get his ranch built back up."

Rosie's lips quirked. "Charles is...well, he's working hard. But he'll get through it. We both will."

"Never doubted it for a second," Mr. Watson replied with a wink. "You two are quite the pair. Like a couple of wild mustangs—takes a bit to rein 'em in, but once you do, there ain't no stopping 'em."

"Thank you, Mr. Watson. That means more to me than you know." Rosie's words were sincere, touched by the truth in his jest.

Leaving the store with her purchases and newfound resolve, Rosie allowed herself to daydream of the moment Charles would finally let his guard down, It wasn't an 'if' but a 'when,' and she would be there—steady and waiting.

For now, she would laugh with him, work beside him, and love him. She would be his sanctuary.

Chapter Eight

Rosie's fingers were chilled to the bone, yet she couldn't help but smile as she stood beside Charles amid the park where they'd decided to hold the Christmas festival. The park was a flurry of activity with townsfolk hammering and hoisting booths into place, their breaths visible puffs in the frosty air.

"First Friday and Saturday of December," Rosie confirmed. "It'll be perfect timing for folks to buy gifts and celebrate."

"It will," Charles replied. He glanced at a parchment in his hands, the list of vendors and attractions. "The booth revenue should be substantial. I'm surprised at the sheer amount of craftspeople we have."

"Plus, with my sisters and I baking up a storm, we'll have a nice little nest egg for the town's expenses." Rosie's thoughts flitted to the mountain of cookies and pies they'd plan to create. "And we can make this a yearly thing with no extra cost to the town because we will have the booths made."

"Ah, don't forget the tree-lighting ceremony." His eyes twinkled with anticipation, a flicker of boyish excitement that rarely surfaced. "And the snowman contest. Many children have told me they intend to win."

Rosie chuckled, imagining the creativity the children would show in the contest. She couldn't wait to be a judge.

Together, they ambled through the park, their boots crunching on the freshly fallen snow that blanketed Hope Springs like a pristine white quilt. Rosie could almost hear the laughter and music that would soon fill the air, the scent of pine and cinnamon heavy on her senses.

"Looks like we might have to spill over into the schoolyard," Charles mused, gesturing toward the space already brimming with booths. "We're running out of room here."

"Isn't that thrilling?" Rosie's heart leapt. The fair was growing. "The children will love having part of the fair right on their playground."

"Thrilling," Charles agreed, the corner of his mouth twitching upward.

"Imagine the schoolyard aglow with lanterns and the sound of carols drifting from the chapel..." Rosie trailed off, lost in the vision of the vibrant celebration.

"Rosie, I believe this Christmas fair will be the most memorable event yet," Charles said.

As they continued their walk, Rosie felt the hope within her grow brighter. She silently prayed that working together would bring her and Charles closer together. She loved the man, and it was time he realized he loved her.

ROSIE'S FOOTSTEPS ECHOED through the empty church as she approached the pastor, who was tidying up the pews. The scent of beeswax and old wood filled the air, mingling with the faintest trace of incense left over from Sunday service. She cleared her throat gently to announce her presence before speaking.

"Pastor?" Her voice sounded steady despite the butterflies in her stomach. "I've come to ask if you'd be willing to announce our Christmas Fair from the pulpit? We're planning it for the first weekend of December."

The pastor looked up from his task, a kind smile softening his features. "Of course, Rosie," he replied, setting aside his cloth. "I'll make sure to mention it two weeks prior, and again the week right before.

I think this is an event that will bring the whole community together. After the sabotage in the mines this year, we need it."

"Thank you so much," Rosie said, relief washing over her. She beamed at him, her gratitude genuine. The fair would need all the town's support to succeed.

Later that afternoon, Rosie found herself in the warm embrace of Ana's kitchen, where the comforting smell of baking bread and cinnamon wafted through the air. Ana and Izzy were gathered around the sturdy oak table.

"All right, ladies," Rosie said, "it's time to discuss the fair. We need to bake, and we need to bake a lot. Every penny counts toward improving the town."

"Can't we just buy the sweets?" Izzy groaned, leaning back in her chair with a dramatic sigh. "You know I turn the kitchen into a disaster every time I try to bake."

Ana rolled her eyes, already donning her apron.

"Fine," Rosie relented with a chuckle, shaking her head at her sister's antics. "But you can't just sit pretty while we do all the work. You have nimble fingers, Izzy. How about you knit some of those lovely socks of yours? They'll sell like hotcakes."

"Knitting I can do," Izzy said, perking up immediately. A triumphant smile curled her lips as she reached for her yarn basket. "I'll make enough socks to warm the toes of half the county!"

"Then it's settled," Rosie declared, smiling at each of her sisters in turn. "We'll fill our booth with the fruits of our labor—be it baked or knitted—and make this fair one to remember. Charles and I have even talked about making this an annual thing."

Rosie lifted baby Lillian into her arms, the tiny bundle of joy squirming with an infectious giggle that tickled Rosie's heart. The little one's eyes sparkled, her chubby fingers clutching at Rosie's blouse as if anchoring herself to this moment of affection. Cradling Lillian close, Rosie's thoughts drifted like snowflakes on a calm winter morn.

She yearned for a child of her own, a sweet life she could hold and cherish, just as she did with Lillian. But the longing in her soul was tempered by the stark reality of her marriage bed. Charles was a good man, but their union lacked the intimacy they needed to start a family.

"Isn't that right, my precious one?" Rosie cooed, brushing a kiss atop Lillian's soft head. "Auntie Rosie would love a little troublemaker like you." The babe responded with a toothless grin, oblivious to the weight of unspoken dreams cradled in her aunt's arms.

With Lillian now settled, Rosie donned her coat and stepped outside. The air was crisp, nipping at her cheeks as she made her way home through Hope Springs, past storefronts adorned with garlands and bows, all preparing for the upcoming Christmas fair.

"Even my sisters," Rosie mused, a bittersweet smile playing on her lips. "Blessings upon blessings, while I..." Rosie shook her head. She couldn't start feeling sorry for herself. It wasn't in her nature.

ROSIE APPROACHED THE entrance of the post office, her breath clouding the chill air. She nodded to Mr. Whitaker behind the counter, his spectacles perched precariously on the bridge of his nose as he squinted at the mail.

"Good afternoon, Rosie," he said, shuffling through the stack of letters with a practiced hand. "Seems there's something here for you and your sisters."

"Thank you, Mr. Whitaker," Rosie replied, accepting the envelope with a polite smile. The script was elegant, the name unfamiliar—curiosity pricked at her, a welcome distraction from the weight of her thoughts. It was addressed to her Ana, and Izzy.

"Any idea who this might be from?" she asked casually, turning the envelope over in her hands.

"Can't say that I do," Mr. Whitaker answered, pushing his glasses up. "We get all sorts of mail here. Could be anyone."

"Of course," Rosie said, tucking the letter into her coat pocket.

Stepping back out into the crisp afternoon, Rosie took the longer path home, winding through the park where children laughed and chased each other, their cheeks rosy from the cold. Their innocent joy was a balm to her soul, and for a moment, she allowed herself to imagine what it would be like to share such laughter with a child of her own.

She walked into the house and realized she had a few minutes before she needed to start supper. Rosie removed her coat and settled into the chair by the hearth, where embers glowed softly beneath the ash. The room was quiet, save for the occasional pop of wood and the whisper of her skirts as she unfolded the mysterious letter.

"Who are you?" she whispered to the name etched on the page, her voice imbued with a mix of anticipation and trepidation. Her fingers traced the loops and flourishes of the handwriting as if they might reveal the secrets hidden within the folds of parchment.

Taking a deep breath, Rosie broke the seal. The paper crackled as she unfolded it, the words awaiting her hungry gaze like the first delicate snowflakes of winter, ready to transform the landscape of her life.

ROSIE'S HANDS MOVED mechanically, stirring the pot of stew that simmered on the stove. Across the kitchen table, Charles was immersed in ledgers and papers, his brows drawn together in concentration as he attended to the business of their small but growing town.

"More salt?" she asked, feeding him a spoonful.

"Uh? Oh, yes, please," Charles replied absentmindedly, not looking up from his work.

She complied, although her thoughts were far from the seasoning of their evening meal. She couldn't stop thinking about the letter. She wanted to share with her sisters immediately, but she wasn't sure if Charles would think less of her if he knew, so she would wait until she saw them the following afternoon.

"Are you feeling quite all right, Rosie?" Charles finally glanced up. "You're quieter than I've ever seen you."

"Merely a headache," she lied, tucking a stray lock of hair behind her ear in a failed attempt at nonchalance. "I'll be fine after some rest."

"Of course," Charles agreed, though his gaze lingered on her for a moment longer before returning to his work.

Dinner passed in silence, save for the clinking of utensils against plates. Rosie pushed her food around, appetite lost to the gnawing curiosity and dread the letter inspired. Charles, ever absorbed in the planning of the Christmas fair, spoke only to outline tasks for the coming days, his voice a distant hum in her ears.

"Goodnight, my dear," Charles said, standing to extinguish the lamps. "Let's hope your head is clearer in the morning."

"Goodnight," Rosie said, her lips curving in a smile that didn't reach her eyes. She climbed the stairs to her bedroom, the weight of the unread words pulling her down with each step.

Once ensconced in bed, the only sound was the rustle of sheets as she withdrew the letter from its hiding place beneath her pillow. Her fingers trembled as she lit the lantern.

With bated breath, Rosie unfolded the letter, holding it close enough that the ink might as well have been etched upon her soul. The lantern's glow flickered across her features as she read the message once more.

Rosie lay awake for hours, thinking about how she would need to share its contents with her sisters the next day, though she wanted to run to them and show them immediately. Their husbands would not approve, she was afraid, and neither would hers.

Chapter Nine

Rosie held Lillian nestled in her arms. Izzy was on the floor, her face a mask of exaggerated enthusiasm as she dangled a knitted rabbit above the baby's head, eliciting gurgles of delight.

"Almost time for Ana to return," Rosie murmured, her gaze shifting between the clock and the letter tucked safely inside her apron pocket. The weight of the unspoken words pressed against her chest, but she remained resolute. She owed it to both her sisters to share the news when they were all together.

Izzy looked up, catching the edge in Rosie's voice. "Everything all right?" she asked, resting back on her heels while keeping one eye on Lillian's flailing hands.

"Fine, just fine," Rosie assured with a swift smile.

"Is it Charles again?" Izzy's brow crinkled with concern.

"No, no, nothing of that sort," Rosie hastened to say, quelling the urge to divulge the contents of the letter. It wasn't the right time—not yet.

The front door creaked open, and there stood Ana, her cheeks flushed from the brisk morning air and her hair escaping the confines of her bun in wispy rebellion. She shed her coat, revealing the subtle swell of pregnancy beneath her dress.

"Goodness, smells like heaven in here," Ana beamed, unwinding the scarf from around her neck.

"Chicken pot pie," Rosie announced, pride lacing her tone. "And apple crisp for dessert."

"Rosie, you spoil us," Ana said as they gathered around the table, clinking their forks against the plates laden with steaming pie. They recounted tales from the infirmary and debated the merits of adding nutmeg to apple desserts.

Once the final crumbs had been swept away, the sisters piled their dishes into the sink. Soapy water sloshed over the sides as Rosie plunged her hands into the suds, passing clean plates to Ana for drying. Izzy, humming a tune, stacked them with precision. They'd done dishes this way together many times over the years, and it felt comfortable.

"Ana, Izzy," Rosie said, "there's something we need to discuss." She dried her hands on her apron.

"Sounds serious," Ana said, matching Rosie's somber expression.

"Yesterday, a letter arrived." Rosie drew the envelope from her pocket, its edges worn from her handling. "It's addressed to all three of us. From Massachusetts."

"Massachusetts?" Izzy repeated, her interest piqued.

"It must be from Elizabeth Tandy!" Ana guessed.

"Let's sit," Rosie suggested, leading them to the sitting area. They perched on the edge of the sofa.

"Before I read it," Rosie took a deep breath, "I want you both to know that whatever it says, we're in this together."

"Always," Ana affirmed, reaching out to squeeze Rosie's hand.

"Of course," Izzy agreed.

With shared nods of encouragement, Rosie broke the seal of the letter, unfolding the future as easily as the creased paper in her hands.

Rosie's hands trembled slightly as she held the letter aloft, the weight of its contents as heavy as lead in her heart. She settled into the high-backed armchair, her eyes glancing over to where Lillian lay, swaddled in dreams. The baby's chest rose and fell in a rhythm that commanded silence and gentleness.

"Shall we?" Izzy whispered, needles poised above the soft blue yarn, a half-finished sock in her lap. Ana, across from her, nodded, her own knitting forgotten for the moment.

"Keep your voices down," Rosie reminded them softly, glancing at Lillian's peaceful face before carefully smoothing out the paper.

She began to read, her voice a hushed murmur that wove around the click-clack of Izzy's knitting needles.

Massachusetts,

October 8, 1898

My Beloved Daughters,

My heart is laden with a multitude of emotions—hope, trepidation, and an overwhelming love—as I endeavor to connect with you, my dear daughters, whom I have yearned to know since I learned of your births.

The story is long, and I hope you will bear with me, as I endeavor to tell it in a way that will not put anyone in a bad light. It begins with a young love, pure and bright, shared between your mother and me in 1876. Our time together was brief but filled with a lifetime's worth of dreams. The night before I joined the army, I asked your mother to be my wife, and she agreed to wait for me.

Upon my return, the world I knew had shifted irrevocably. Your mother, whom I loved dearly, had faced unimaginable hardships, and made choices that she believed were best for her future, and yours as well. It was then I learned of your existence, three precious lives born from the night I asked her to marry me, that I wished I'd not left her alone. I became but a shadow in your lives, wishing that I could be with you as I learned that another had taken my role as Miranda's husband and your father.

The man you have known as your father, I have come to understand, bore a tempest within him, one that oftentimes cast shadows over your lives and that of your mother's. Your mother's choice to stay, driven by circumstances and fierce love for her daughters told me of her strength—a strength I see mirrored in all of you, even from afar.

Today, I reach out not just as a man who once loved your mother, but as a father who has silently held you in his heart, cherished and loved from the moment I learned of your existence. The truth of your parentage changes nothing of your value. I hope there is a future where we can explore what it means to be a family.

I extend to you an invitation, born from a deep longing to right the silent wrongs of the past, to join me in Massachusetts. Here, we can forge new memories, build new bridges, and perhaps find healing in the telling and retelling of our stories.

It is an offering of love, an outstretched hand, and an open heart, waiting, hoping for the chance to be a part of your lives.

With all the love and hope that fills my heart,

Your Father,

Malcolm Ward

Rosie fell silent as the last word hung in the air, her fingers clutching the letter like a lifeline. For a moment, time itself seemed to pause, allowing the enormity of what they'd just learned to settle upon them.

Izzy dropped her needles, the soft thud on the rug barely audible. "Never our father... " she murmured, more to herself than anyone else.

Ana's brow was furrowed, the line between her eyebrows deepening as she processed the news. "To think all these years," she said, her voice quivering with emotion, "we were raised by a man who didn't share our blood. And now, to discover there's someone out there...who might actually love us."

"Someone who has always loved us," Rosie corrected gently.

"Does this mean we're not who we thought we were?" Izzy asked.

"No, it does not change who we are," Rosie stated firmly. "We are still the women we've grown to be—strong, independent, caring. This...this just adds another layer to our story."

"Another layer," Ana echoed, her gaze distant. "A father who loves us...it's strange to consider. Like discovering a hidden chapter in a book you thought you knew by heart."

"Exactly," Rosie said, a wry smile touching her lips. "And what an interesting chapter it promises to be."

The sisters sat in contemplative silence, each lost in their own thoughts about what they'd learned.

A tear slipped down Rosie's cheek, unchecked and soon joined by others. Izzy sniffled beside her, a damp spot darkening the yarn in her lap. Ana, ever the nurturer, reached out with trembling hands, placing one on each of her sisters' shoulders as her own eyes brimmed with tears.

"Hope Springs is our home now. We can't just leave," Rosie said, her voice cracking with emotion.

"Going back to Massachusetts would be like stepping backward into the unknown," Izzy murmured.

Ana nodded in agreement. "Our roots are here. Our future is here." She rubbed her belly subconsciously, thinking of the new life growing within her.

"Then we'll invite him here," Rosie declared, wiping her eyes with the back of her hand. "He should see us in our element, where we've flourished despite everything."

"Where we've found love and built our families," added Izzy.

"Exactly." Rosie stood resolutely, the emotional storm giving way to a quiet determination. "Let's write to him together."

The three women gathered around the table. With a fresh sheet of paper before them, they composed their invitation, each sister contributing her own touch.

"Dear Father," Rosie began, her penmanship steady and sure.

"Know that we received your letter with an array of emotions," Ana continued.

"And while it was unexpected, we find ourselves thrilled to know there is a man who has cared for us all this time," Izzy added.

"Please, come to Hope Springs. It would give us great joy to meet you," Rosie wrote.

"Ana is expecting, and so is Izzy," she added, pride lacing her words. "And I'm busy with preparations for the Christmas fair—a true highlight of our town."

"Hope Springs is a place of new beginnings, of second chances," Ana said softly, her gaze distant yet hopeful. "It would mean the world to us if you could share in the life we've built here."

"We hope you can find your way to visiting us here," they concluded together, signing their names.

As Rosie folded the letter with care, the weight of their shared hope settled over the room.

"Imagine," Izzy said, "Our father coming to Hope Springs. He won't know what hit him!"

Rosie couldn't help but chuckle, even as her heart swelled with anticipation. "I think he'll be surprised. But more than anything, he'll see how his daughters have grown strong, even without his love in our lives."

"Strong, beautiful, and utterly indomitable," Ana added, the corners of her mouth lifting in a smile that reflected not just amusement but a profound love for the sisters beside her.

At home that evening, Rosie explained to Charles about her behavior of the night before. "I didn't want you to think less of me, knowing that my sisters and I were conceived out of wedlock, but we decided to tell you, William, and Albert."

Charles nodded. "I think that's the best news you could have received. I don't think any less of you. I knew that you're strong despite your upbringing. I can only imagine how strong you'd be if he'd been in your life."

Rosie smiled and scooted across the couch until she was in Charles's embrace. His words had made her feel so much more confident in her future.

ROSIE CARRIED THE TELEGRAM received to Ana's house. Her sisters leaned in closer, their knitted brows mirroring her own as she unfolded the missive. The parlor was quiet except for Rosie's voice.

"December second," Rosie read aloud, her voice steady but her heart pounding like a drumbeat against her chest. "He's coming on December second."

Ana smiled. "That's the first day of the fair!" she exclaimed.

Izzy nodded. "We'll have to make sure everything is perfect for his arrival," she said.

Rosie felt the weight of responsibility settle upon her shoulders, not just for the success of the Christmas fair she'd poured her soul into organizing, but now also for ensuring their father's visit was memorable.

"Let's take turns showing him around," Rosie suggested, already picturing the schedule in her mind. "The fair will be busy, but we can each steal away a little time with him."

"Agreed," Izzy chimed in. "And he can stay at my place. Albert won't mind, and it's spacious enough for privacy."

"Will there be room for all the stories we have to share?" Ana joked.

"Plenty," Izzy assured, her eyes twinkling with warmth. "After all, what is a home without tales of love and hardship, laughter and tears?"

As they discussed the logistics, Rosie's passion for the fair mingled with a newfound desire to connect with the man who had unknowingly shaped their destinies.

"Hope Springs is about to show our father the true meaning of Christmas," Rosie declared, her eyes alight with fierce determination. "And I dare say, no daughter of his could do otherwise."

Their laughter filled the room, a chorus of joy and anticipation for the season of giving, the celebration of community, and the wondrous revelation of family rediscovered.

THE FIRST GOLDEN RAYS of dawn had barely graced the bustling town of Hope Springs when the long-awaited train arrived. Rosie's heart hammered in her chest as she watched a tall, distinguished gentleman step down from the carriage, his eyes scanning the crowd until they came to rest on her and her sisters. Beside him emerged a woman, her elegant poise unmistakable even from a distance.

"Ana, Izzy," Rosie whispered, clutching their hands as they stood shoulder to shoulder, "he's here."

Ana's fiery curls seemed to bounce with her nerves, and Izzy smoothed the front of her dress, an unconscious gesture for composure. As the pair approached, Rosie took a deep breath, steadying herself to be the voice of welcome.

"Mr. Malcolm Ward, I presume?" Rosie extended her hand. "And you must be Mrs. Ward? We're honored by your visit."

"Call me Father," he said, his voice rich and resonant, enveloping her in an embrace that warmed her through. "And this is my wife, Carrie."

"Rosie," she introduced herself, then gestured to Ana and Izzy. "And these are my sisters, Anabelle and Isabelle."

"Such lovely names for such lovely young women," Mrs. Ward chimed in, her smile genuine and kind.

"Thank you, ma'am," Izzy replied, her voice a soft melody of politeness.

"Please, call me Carrie," she insisted.

"Father," Rosie said, eager to fill the silence that followed introductions, "we've planned quite a day for the town fair. There'll be booths selling all manner of crafts and goods, games for the children, and food—so much food!" She spoke with the fervor of someone who had poured her soul into the event. "We thought it best to take turns accompanying you, so each of us can share a bit of our lives here in Hope Springs with you."

"Sounds delightful," Malcolm said, his eyes twinkling with interest.

"Speaking of which," Carrie interjected, her gaze sweeping over the colorful array of stands dotting the fairground, "I would love to help the three of you with your booth. Then you can spend a little more time with Malcolm."

"Truly?" Izzy's surprise was evident. "That would be most appreciated, Carrie."

"Excellent!" Carrie clapped her hands together, a burst of enthusiasm escaping her. "Let's not waste another moment then. Lead the way!"

As Rosie guided their father through the fair, pointing out the various attractions, her mind was ablaze with thoughts. Here was a man connected to them by blood, yet he was as much a mystery as any other stranger.

"Here's our booth," Ana said. They had arrived at the stand adorned with baked goods and knitted wares.

"Allow me to show you how it's done," Carrie said, pulling on her gloves with a grin that mirrored the gleam of excitement in Ana's eyes. It was as if the stepmother they had just met was already welcoming them into her life.

Rosie watched from the corner of her eye as Izzy and Ana, each with their husbands by their sides, approached Malcolm and Carrie.

"Malcolm, Carrie, this is my husband, Albert," Izzy said with a modest pride that resonated in her voice. Albert Thoreau's stature was commanding, his presence a testament to his success, but in front of Malcolm, there was an uncharacteristic boyishness about him.

"An absolute pleasure," Albert extended a firm handshake to Malcolm. "Your daughters have become dear to this town, and you should be proud."

"They are remarkable women," Malcolm replied. Beside him, Carrie nodded, her smile a perfect curve of warmth and acceptance.

"And this is William," Ana chimed in, gesturing to Dr. Mercer who had been hanging back slightly. "My husband and our town's physician."

"Doctor," Malcolm greeted, clasping William's hand. "I understand we owe you a great debt for looking after our girls here."

"Sir, it has been my honor," William said. "They've looked after me just as much."

Laughter rippled through the gathering. Rosie was proud of what she and her sisters had accomplished in the months since their mother's death.

"Rosie, aren't you going to introduce Charles?" Ana asked, turning toward her with a teasing glint in her eye.

"Ah, yes," Rosie murmured, her gaze lingering on the fair's bustling entrance where she knew her meticulous plans were springing to life. "Charles will be along shortly. Town matters, you know how it is."

"Of course," Malcolm said with a knowing nod. "The mayor's work is never done."

"Exactly," Rosie agreed, her lips twitching into a wry smile. "But I'll ensure he doesn't miss out on meeting you."

"Take your time, Rosie," Carrie said. "We'll be here when you're ready."

"Thank you, Carrie," Rosie said, touched by the kindness in her stepmother's voice. It was a strange thing, feeling tethered to these near strangers.

"Besides," Rosie continued, her gaze dancing across the fairground alive with eager townsfolk and vibrant colors, "I've put my heart into this fair. I want to see it unfold from the start. You'll understand when you see it, Father. We all need to get into our booths because the fair is finally starting!"

"Father." It felt strange to look into this kind man's face and equate him with the word, but it had never seemed to fit Mr. Winslow, whom she would never think of as a father again.

"Then let's make sure this fair is one for the history books, shall we?" Malcolm declared.

"This is what I've been working toward for months. It needs to be in the history books!" Rosie said, determination lighting her features.

Rosie felt a surge of anticipation for the day ahead. It was a beginning, not just for the fair, but for the family they were only just starting to build.

Rosie's hands danced over the few remaining pairs of socks at their booth. Thankfully, they had more at Ana's house, and it was just a matter of running to get them.

"Rosie, you've outdone yourself," Malcolm's voice broke through the noise as he approached.

"Thank you, Father," she said. "Hope Springs has never seen a fair quite like this one."

Most of the baked goods were gone, and she knew there would be a great deal of baking that evening. Perhaps even Carrie would join them. The woman seemed to have an endless supply of energy after that long train ride.

"Would you care for a walk? I'm famished, and I hear Mrs. Beasley's meat pies are not to be missed," Malcolm suggested, gesturing toward the food vendors who were still bustling with activity.

"Absolutely," Rosie agreed, securing the money box beneath the counter before stepping out from behind the booth. She watched as Malcolm confidently navigated the throng, heading straight for the stand where golden-crusted pies sat temptingly on display.

"Two meat pies, please," he ordered, handing Rosie one wrapped in a square of brown paper that felt warm against her skin.

"Father, let me show you around." Rosie took a bite of the flaky pastry, savoring the peppery filling that warmed her from inside out. They strolled side by side, her pointing out various attractions: the children's laughter ringing from the makeshift carousel Dr. Mercer had engineered, the choir singing carols off-key but with unmistakable joy, and the miners competing in an arm-wrestling contest, their muscles bulging as they battled for bragging rights.

"Over there," she said between bites, indicating a group of women gathered around a quilt they were stitching together, "that's the community quilt. Each family adds a square. By next year, it'll be large enough to cover the mayor's house!"

Malcolm chuckled, his eyes crinkling at the corners. "I should hope Charles has no objections to such an ornate covering."

"Charles knows better than to argue with tradition," Rosie quipped, her heart light despite the lingering thoughts of her husband's aloofness. Today was about celebration, about family—both old and new.

"The whole town has pulled together in a way I couldn't have imagined for this event." Rosie said, her words laced with a passion that mirrored the vibrant life of the fair around them. "And now, you're a part of it too."

"Rosie," Malcolm said, "you've done a beautiful job here. I'm so proud of you!"

She met his gaze, noticing a familiar determination there that mirrored her own. "Thank you, Father," Rosie said, her heart swelling with a mix of pride and anticipation for the future. "But we're just getting started."

The meat pie in her hand was half-eaten, its savory warmth a comfort against the chill that crept into the air. As she and Malcolm walked in step, Rosie couldn't help but feel a magnetic pull toward her father.

"Your mother," Malcolm began, his voice faltering with an emotion Rosie hadn't expected to see in him, "she had a laugh that could light up the darkest room." His smile waned, replaced by a somber tightness around his eyes. "I'm sorry, truly sorry, for what you girls had to endure growing up. I would've done things differently if only I'd known."

Rosie glanced at him, seeing the regret etching lines deeper into his face.

"I think we're just relieved that we aren't related to Mr. Winslow. You've obviously heard some of the stories. You came at just the right time." She paused for a moment. "I may take you up on the offer of a visit. With Ana and Izzy expecting, I know they won't, but I'll talk to Charles tonight." Perhaps he'd be happy to see her go. It felt like the right thing to do, and having a father with her would help her.

Malcolm nodded, a look of relief softening his features. They continued to walk through the fair, passing children laughing as they played games and couples strolling arm in arm. Rosie pointed out each attraction, describing how it contributed to the community and the joy of Hope Springs.

"Charles really should be here to see this," Malcolm observed, watching a young couple dance to a fiddler's lively tune.

Rosie's smile didn't quite reach her eyes. "He's ensuring everything runs smoothly elsewhere," she replied, her cheeks coloring with a hint of frustration.

"Ah, the burden of leadership," Malcolm mused. "It can make you forget to live a little."

"Perhaps," Rosie conceded.

As the fair began to wind down, Rosie felt a sense of accomplishment; the booth was nearly bare, her efforts having paid off. They had sold off many of the socks, and she would work on baking more that night.

"Thank you for today, for everything," Rosie said, her gaze meeting Malcolm's once more.

"Thank you for inviting me into your life, Rosie," he replied, clasping her hands in his.

"Do you think I could borrow Carrie this evening? We're completely out of baked goods, and I want to have something to offer the people who couldn't make it today. One more day, and this is done!"

Her father nodded. "I think that would be wonderful. I wouldn't mind coming and spending the evening with Charles."

"Of course!" Rosie said. "Let's find her and I'll walk you to my home. I'm sure either Charles or I will be happy to walk you to Izzy's when we're finished. Izzy has the most beautiful house, and that's where you'll be staying."

"Yes, Albert took our things there earlier, but we have yet to see it."

As they walked toward the ranch, Rosie's mind was on Charles and approaching him about going home with her father. He didn't seem to want her around most of the time, so it would be a good solution.

Chapter Ten

Rosie's sleeves were rolled up to her elbows, and flour covered the apron tied snugly around her waist. She shaped the dough into whimsical shapes, her hands deft and practiced. Carrie stood beside her at the counter, her more delicate fingers carefully adding frosting to a batch of cookies.

"Rosie," Carrie said, "I never did have children of my own. You can't imagine how it warms my heart to finally include Malcolm's daughters as part of my family." She glanced up from her meticulous work, her eyes glistening. "I'm so happy you're letting me help with this and be a part of your life."

Rosie paused, her hands stilling on the pastry. She looked over at Carrie, seeing the genuine joy etched into her features. "I'm so glad, Carrie. We're blessed to have you in our lives too," Rosie said sincerely. "Our mother was good to us in every way. When the man we thought was our father said we couldn't go to church, Mother read scripture to us and prayed with us. When he said we couldn't go to school, she taught us to read, write, and do arithmetic. She taught us history. She let us go to the stream in the summer so we could cool off. She broke many of his rules for us. The only thing she didn't do was tell us that we had another father who loved us." Rosie shook her head. "I can't love her any less for it because I saw her take many beatings that were meant for me and my sisters. How could I blame her for anything? Do I wish we'd had both of our parents our entire lives? In more ways than I can say. Am I angry with her for it? No. We don't need a mother in our lives in the same way we need a father, but we are all pleased to welcome a new one into our lives."

As the evening wore on, the kitchen table became laden with an assortment of baked goods, each more inviting than the last.

Finally, Malcolm and Carrie donned their coats and prepared to leave. They shared satisfied smiles as they surveyed the bounty laid out before them. Rosie stepped into Carrie's arms. "Thank you so much for helping our little town with me. You have no idea how much I enjoyed spending this time with you."

"Thank you for this evening," Malcolm said, his voice rich with gratitude. Carrie took his arm, and together, along with Charles, they stepped out into the crisp night air.

After returning from walking his in-laws to Albert's house, Charles appeared in the doorway of the kitchen, leaning against the frame. He watched Rosie as she tidied up, her movements efficient yet graceful.

"Rosie," he said, catching her attention. She turned to him. "Today was a resounding success. And your father, he's quite a man. Kindness seems to run in the family."

Before Rosie could respond, Charles closed the distance between them and gently kissed her cheek. It was a simple gesture, but it sent a flutter through her heart.

"Goodnight, Rosie," Charles said softly, his gaze lingering on hers just a moment longer than necessary. He quickly went up to bed, leaving her touching her cheek where his lips had been.

Rosie hesitated outside Charles's bedroom door, her fingers trembling as they traced the wood grain before she rapped softly.

Inside, Charles sat on the edge of his bed, elbows on knees. His posture spoke volumes, the weight of the world seemingly perched upon his broad shoulders.

"Charles?"

He looked up and there was no mistaking the surprise in his eyes as he met her gaze. "Rosie? Is everything all right?"

"May I?" She gestured to the space beside him.

"Of course." He straightened, making room for her.

Rosie sat and turned to face him. "Charles, I've been thinking," she began. "Perhaps...it would be best if I went back to Massachusetts with Malcolm and Carrie. I can't help but feel that I'm not what you wanted in a wife."

"Rosie," he stammered, looking surprised, "why would you say such a thing?"

"Because," she whispered, "you seem so far away, even when you're right beside me."

"Rosie," Charles said. "I think you're perfect. Everything about you—the way you care for others, your strength, your laughter—it's more than I ever hoped for."

"Then why—" she started, but he placed a finger over her lips, silencing her.

"Because," he said, "I have been distant, and it's not fair to you. It's just that..."

"Charles, if we are to make this work, we must be honest with each other," Rosie said, her hand covering his. "I want us to be real, to share every part of our lives, not just live under the same roof as strangers."

"Rosie," Charles whispered. "You deserve that. We both do."

"Then let's start now," Rosie urged.

Charles paced the room. "Rosie," he finally said, "I think I owe you more than I've told you."

"What haven't you told me?" she asked.

"Rosie," Charles began, "I've been carrying burdens I haven't wanted to share. But seeing you, knowing you...it makes me want to try. To try and let go of those fears that have shackled me."

Rosie reached out, her hand finding his.

"Tell me, Charles," she whispered. "I'm right here with you. And I'm not going anywhere."

"Rosie," he began, "my late wife did everything she could to control me. If I did something that made her happy, she would allow me to have marital relations with her. If we fought, there would be no relations."

Rosie watched him, her eyes warm and comforting.

"Every day was difficult. I loved her, but she killed that love rather quickly." A pained chuckle escaped him. "When she passed from pneumonia, it was as though the air cleared for the first time in years. And I felt guilt for feeling that relief, Rosie."

In the flickering light, Rosie's hand reached out, finding his arm. He had to know he had her unwavering support. "Charles," she said, "there's no shame in feeling relief at her death. I felt relief when my mother died, not only because she'd been ill, but because it meant my sisters and I could leave there."

Charles nodded.

"Your heart, it's been through the wringer, but here you are—opening up to me," Rosie continued. "That takes more courage than most men can muster. I'm here for you, Charles, to stand by your side and help you in any way I can."

A mix of emotions swirled within him. The laughter that bubbled up now held a trace of genuine mirth, born from the absurdity of finding solace in the heart of a woman who was supposed to be nothing more than a means to an end.

THEIR KISS WAS SLOW at first, but quickly became passionate. Clothes were shed, fluttering to the wooden floor of his bedroom. As they came together, the warmth of their bodies entwined, she understood the magic her sisters had talked about that happened with their husbands.

Afterward, as he held her, Charles whispered, "I love you so much, Rosie."

Rosie lifted her head and looked into his face. "I love you, Charles. I don't believe I could express how much."

THE FOLLOWING EVENING at Izzy and Albert's house, the air was thick with the scent of roasted meat and freshly baked bread. Laughter and conversation bubbled around them, but Charles found himself with his gaze anchored to Rosie. She was radiant, her cheeks flushed with a rosy hue that matched her name.

"Charles?" Albert nudged him gently. "You planning to join us here anytime soon, or is the view from whatever cloud you're on too enchanting to leave?"

"Apologies, Albert," Charles replied with a sheepish grin, tearing his eyes away from Rosie for a fleeting moment. "It seems I've discovered something worth getting lost in."

"Ah, love," Albert mused, clinking his glass lightly against Charles's. "Makes even the most grounded of men float away."

"Yes," William chimed in from across the table, raising his own glass in salute. "To floating away."

As the night unfolded, Charles savored each glance exchanged with Rosie, each subtle touch beneath the tablecloth, all the while marveling at how vastly his world had expanded since allowing his emotions to surface.

LATER, AFTER THE LAUGHTER from the dinner table had dwindled into a contented murmur, Malcolm sat with his hands clasped, his gaze flitting across the faces of his daughters and their husbands.

"Girls," he began, his voice catching slightly. "Carrie and I have been talking, and there's something we need to share."

Rosie felt a flutter in her chest. She exchanged a quick, searching glance with her sisters, Ana's fiery curls bobbing as she leaned in, Izzy's elegant poise unshaken but her eyes alight with curiosity.

"Carrie and I..." Malcolm continued. "We've grown quite fond of this place, of being here with you all. The thought of returning to Massachusetts without you is more than we can bear." He paused, looking down at his weathered hands before meeting their eyes again. "Would you mind terribly...if we decided to settle here, close to our family?"

For a moment, the room was silent. Then, as if by some unspoken signal, the Winslow sisters turned to each other, their expressions a complex tapestry of joy, surprise, and an inkling of mischief that only siblings could share.

"Yes," they answered in unison.

"Truly?" Malcolm's eyes misted over.

"Of course, Father," Rosie said, her voice warm with affection. "This town could use more good people like you and Carrie."

"Besides," Ana chimed in, her grin wide and impish, "Hope Springs has never seen a batch of cookies quite like Carrie's. You'll both fit right in."

"And it will be good for Lillian to grow up with a grandfather close by. And the babies on their way," Izzy added softly.

"Seems Hope Springs is quite the magnet," Charles remarked. "Attracting all sorts of treasures."

"Very true," William agreed, his tone carrying the weight of his medical wisdom. "I've always said, 'Family is the best medicine.'"

"Especially when it comes with Carrie's cookies," Albert said.

"Then it's settled," Malcolm said, his voice buoyant with relief and newfound purpose. "Hope Springs, prepare for two more eager hearts to call you home."

Epilogue

Ten Years later

Rosie stood in the middle of a gathering in Albert and Izzy's parlor. "Look at this," Charles said, sidling up to Rosie. "Who would've thought?"

She smiled at him. They had weathered storms together, braved uncertainties, and now they basked in the comfort of enduring love—a love that had only grown stronger with each passing year.

Rosie sighed contentedly, leaning into Charles. His arm wrapped around her waist, anchoring her against him.

The afternoon was a true success, with the entire family gathered together. Rosie couldn't help but reflect on the immeasurable ways their lives had intertwined, creating memories and shared history.

"Hope Springs really is our little sanctuary," she murmured to Charles, her words barely audible above the din.

He nodded, his eyes meeting hers with an intensity that made her heart flutter even now. "Our sanctuary," he echoed, "built on the foundation of love, passion, and a dash of good old-fashioned stubbornness."

"Wouldn't have it any other way," Rosie said, her heart full as she surveyed the room—the place where their past met their future, a future they were all crafting together, one heartfelt moment at a time.

Charles watched as a whirlwind of children swirled through Izzy and Albert's parlor. Each set of twins, products of the remarkable fertility that seemed to run in his wife's family seemed happier than the last.

"Eleven sets," Charles muttered under his breath, marveling at the sheer number of little ones. "And not a single one flying solo other than Lillian."

"Surprised, dear?" Rosie's voice pulled him from his thoughts. She sidled up beside him, her belly rounded with the promise of yet another duo.

"Every day," he confessed, turning to meet her gaze. "I thought I'd signed up for a quiet life, but I seem to have enlisted in an army of ankle-biters instead."

Rosie's hand found his, squeezing gently. "Just be happy only three sets of twins are ours. Well, four soon," she said with a knowing smile.

"I don't know how William does it. Nine children with two more on the way," he agreed.

The clamor of children crescendoed as they tore through the room once more, their excitement palpable. They converged around Malcolm and Carrie, the patriarch and matriarch of this burgeoning clan, who welcomed each embrace with open arms.

"Looks like the troops are rallying around the generals," Charles observed.

"Or seeking reinforcements," Rosie added, her eyes following the trail of giggles and squeals weaving through the furniture.

"Reinforcements indeed," Charles sighed, shaking his head in mock defeat. "With your sister Ana and William adding to the fray, and Izzy and Albert not far behind, it seems Hope Springs will need to expand its borders just to accommodate the lot of us."

"Expansion is a sign of prosperity," Rosie said, not at all worried about how he felt about the children. He loved the whole lot of them.

"Prosperity," Charles said. "We're rich in ways I never could've counted."

"Rich in love," Rosie corrected softly.

"So rich in love," he agreed as he watched their children tumble into yet another round of hide-and-seek, their laughter echoing through the house like a benediction. "In love and passion, we are beyond wealthy."

"Speaking of which," Rosie leaned in closer, her words for his ears alone, "this next batch might just tip us into outright extravagance."

"Extravagance?" he repeated. "Now that's a currency I can get behind."

Rosie laughed, the sound mingling with the joyous cacophony around them. In that moment, Charles knew that no matter how full their home became, there would always be room for more—more love, more laughter, and yes, even more twins.

CARRIE'S HANDS CRADLED the small child with an innate tenderness. The little one, with tufts of golden hair escaping her bonnet, looked at the other children as if she were the most important person in the world. When one of them had Grandmama's attention, they felt as if they ruled the place.

Across the parlor, Malcolm held another of the brood—a rambunctious toddler who was more intent on wiggling out of his grandfather's hold than staying put. Malcolm's face broke into a smile each time the child let out a peal of laughter.

"Never thought I'd be doing this at my age," Malcolm said, his voice warm with unspoken gratitude. He shifted the child to his other hip, eyes scanning the room filled with the fruits of his daughters' unions. "But here I am, feeling like the richest man in Colorado."

A comfortable silence settled among them before Malcolm cleared his throat.

"I want to thank all of you for allowing Carrie and me into your lives," he began, his tone solemn yet sincere. "I know I wasn't a father, not after leaving you girls to be raised by..." His voice trailed off, unable to summon the name of their stepfather.

"Papa," Rosie interjected. "You're here now. That's what matters."

"We're so happy you're here," Charles added, standing beside his wife, his demeanor supportive. "We are a family now, one that looks forward, not back."

Malcolm nodded, the lines around his eyes softening as he looked at Carrie. "We're grateful," he said.

Rosie caught the wistful undertone in Malcolm's voice. She crossed the room with grace, the bustle of children and laughter of their kinfolk fading into the background. Her heart, always so attuned to the undercurrents of emotion, recognized the moment for what it was—an opportunity to heal old wounds.

"Papa," Rosie said, "you mustn't carry that burden any longer." She reached out, placing a gentle hand on Malcolm's arm, her touch grounding.

Malcolm looked down at her, the sadness in his eyes a stark contrast to the mirth around them. Rosie continued, "We wouldn't be who we are today—strong, and capable of great love—if our past had been any different."

A soft chuckle escaped her lips, not mocking but rather reflecting the irony of life's unpredictable tapestry. "Imagine that! We Winslow girls were toughened by hardship, which allowed us to have the courage to be matched with these stubborn men of Hope Springs."

The corner of Charles's mouth quirked up in response, an affectionate glint in his eye. He stood slightly behind Rosie, his presence a silent pillar of support.

"Rosie is right," Charles said. "Our paths led us here, to this very moment, to the love we've found and the family we've built. Everything truly happens as it's meant to."

Rosie smiled, knowing that everyone here loved her as much as she loved them. Who would have thought triplets who led such horrible childhoods could be so happy?